The Feast of the Lotus

The Feast of the Lotus

Caroline Smith

Copyright © 2024 by Caroline Smith

Published in the United States by Sisters Three Publishing, LLC. All rights reserved. No part of this book may be reproduced, scanned, or transmitted in any printed, electronic, or mechanical, including photocopying, recording, or any information storage and retrieval system, without permission in writing from the publisher. Please do not participate in or encourage piracy of copyrighted materials in violation of the author's rights.

The Feast of the Lotus is a work of fiction. Names, characters, places, and incidents are the products of the author's imagination or are used fictitiously. Any resemblance to actual events, locales, or persons, living or dead, is entirely coincidental.

ISBN: 979-8-3303-4663-9

Printed in the United States of America

Books By Caroline Smith

Fiction

Under a Blanket of Blue

Shadows in the South: A Short Story Collection

The Feast of the Lotus

The Oracle of Magnolia Place (coming fall 2025)

Nonfiction

Writing as Meditation

Perspective Parenting

The souls on earth will do what they desire, and the soul of [the deceased] will go forth at Ra's desire.

— from *The Book of the Dead*, spell 29B

Author's Note

Dear reader. Thank you for considering this book. I've wanted to write a book about Egypt since my grandparents returned from a trip there in the nineties. I was completely captivated by the culture and stories of their travels. If you've picked this book up, that may mean that you have some knowledge of or interest in ancient Egypt or maybe none. Or, maybe one of your favorite movies, like mine, is the 1999 classic, *The Mummy* with Brendan Fraser and Rachel Weisz. Either way, ancient Egyptian mythology is as wild and varied as it's many centuries of dynasties. Most of the history in this book is on the 18th dynasty of the New Kingdom (1550-1069 BCE). I have taken a few liberties, this is a paranormal romance, after all, but I've tried to stay as close to the research and history as I could.

Below, I've included some helpful terms and a brief description of some of the Gods and Goddesses of the Egyptian pantheon that are included in this story, as well as a few of their relevant mythologies.

As far as a content warning, you should know that our MMC is a slightly possessive dead guy. There is also grief over the loss of parents. Death features prominently in this story, as it's hard to tell a story of ancient Egypt without reverence for the world they believed existed as an afterlife. Should any of those topics be problematic, please feel free to skip this book. Otherwise, I hope you enjoy Elisa and Neferamun's story as much as I've enjoyed writing it.

USEFUL TERMS AND PEOPLE:

Shabti figures (also known as *shawbti* and *ushabti*) – Small, carved funerary figurines that are found in tombs, often made of stone, wood, or faience and inscribed with spells or the deceased's name.

Ka – the first part of what was believed to be the soul. This was a person's life force or double that exited the body at death.

Ba – The second part of the soul, which could travel between worlds at death.

Akh – The third part of the soul, often meaning spirit.

Book of the Dead – A manual for the afterworld. Contains spells that were thought to be said by priests during the mummification process to help the deceased enter and navigate the afterworld.

Bastet – The goddess of beauty and love. Often depicted as a cat.

Sekhmet – The second aspect and chaotic side of Bastet in warrior and protector form. Often depicted as a lioness.

Maat – The goddess of truth and justice. Often takes the form of an ostrich feather. She is what the deceased's heart was weighed against to enter the afterworld.

Isis – The main female deity of the Egyptian pantheon. Wife and sister to Osiris and mother to Horus and Bastet. She is the goddess of kinship, protection of the kingdom, magic, and wisdom. She is said to have more magical powers than any other deity.

Osiris – The god of the afterlife, resurrection, fertility, agriculture, and vegetation. The first to be associated with mummification. His brother, Set, cut him up and hid pieces of him all over Egypt; Isis retrieved these pieces, then wrapped him in linen, resurrecting him and enabling him to return to life. Presides over the judgment of the dead in the afterworld.

Horus – God of kings, the sky, healing, and protection. Often depicted with the head of a falcon.

Ammit – "The Devourer" or "Devourer of the Dead." A female deity, often depicted with the head of a crocodile, the forelegs of a lion, and the hindquarters of a hippopotamus. If the deceased's heart was heavier than Maat (the feather of truth), Ammit would eat the heart and the deceased would not be able to have a peaceful eternity.

Apep – God of darkness, disorder, and chaos. The opposition of Maat and the enemy of Ra. Often depicted as a serpent. The myth of Ra and Apep says that because Apep hates the light and the sun (Ra) he chases Ra each day but cannot ever catch him.

Ra – The Lightbringer; god of the sun. God of the sky, the earth, and the afterlife. Also the god of order and kings. Often depicted with the head of a falcon. In the New Kingdom, he was merged with the god Amun and became Amun-Ra.

Chapter One

"Ah, Dr. Kent. So nice to see you." Atef took Elisa Kent's hand and in the custom she'd started growing used to and kissed her on both cheeks. "I hope I haven't kept you waiting."

"No, not at all," she swiped her sweaty palm on her pant leg. "I was just admiring your Tut," she gestured with the same hand in a movement that took in the fifty-foot-tall statue of King Tut in the massive foyer.

Dr. Atef Tawfik smiled kindly at her, the creases of his eyes wrinkling behind his frameless glasses. "Well, now, he's yours, too. Please, follow me."

They walked in step to the very rear of the building and into an elevator that took them several floors down. They chatted about her flight and how she was settling in.

"You've been to Cairo before, yes? With your parents, I think."

Her smile was a little sad. "I have, yes, when I was a little girl before they passed. I've also done a few seasons at Saqqara and Thebes."

"I was sorry to hear of their accident," Atef mentioned the accident as if it had happened yesterday and not sixteen years ago. He paused awkwardly and fumbled for something else to change the subject. "I, uh, remember your experience from your resume. I quite enjoyed your lecture on identification of unknown mummies. Even I learned something." He held his arm in front of the elevator door for her to go before him.

"Just down the hall to your left."

The "hall" was a massively wide white corridor with steel doors and keypads. Obviously, the Grand Egyptian Museum, GEM for short, took their security protocols seriously.

He stopped at a door and swiped a key card followed by a four-digit code. The latch clicked and the room before her was a mass of white walls and filing cabinets and shelves organized within an inch of their life. It was cavernous with tall ceilings, four large tables, and lab equipment set up along the walls. Seeing it all made Elisa tingle with anticipation.

She breathed it in. It smelled like history. Resins, oils, disinfectant, and old linen. Some might have called it musty, but it was a heady perfume to her.

"Welcome home." Atef walked beside her to the nearest table. "Everything you need is in here. We have a laptop and cell phone for you, access cards and codes, and a team at your disposal to help with any moving of heavy objects you might need. There are paper copies of the protocols in that notebook and digital versions on the laptop. You have an office upstairs if you need it, but as you'll be cataloging, I thought you might want to start down here."

"It's perfect."

Atef wasn't kidding when he'd mentioned the state-of-the-art labs in the offer letter he'd sent to her. The labs she had worked in during her internship had been cramped in forgotten basements. As a funerary archeologist and Egyptologist, she preferred to work in the field, but this was the next best thing—history and modern technology working seamlessly together.

"We have a café upstairs. The coffee is delicious. If you're ready, I can take you upstairs to your office."

"Actually, I'd rather go ahead and get started if that's all right."

If Atef was surprised by this, he didn't show it. "Certainly. There are lab coats and gloves in the cabinet. We do dual documentation in the notebooks and then in the database, so we have duplicates of everything." He hesitated, seeming unsure what to say. "You will have an assistant if you'd like one, but we've had a hard time keeping any one on this particular project."

"I know the translations from this dynasty can be a little tricky, so I'm not surprised."

"No, it's not that. They've...well...the four Egyptologists we had before...they went a little...mad a few days in. Three of them quit."

Elisa looked at him, startled. "You didn't mention that in your email. What happened to the fourth?"

"He died. Heart attack."

Her mouth gaped and she closed it abruptly, then cleared her throat. "I see."

"Some of the workers think there may be a curse on this particular sarcophagus."

Elisa smiled. "Well, Atef. I don't believe in curses."

He looked at her blandly when he replied. "Perhaps you should."

With that, he turned toward the door. "I'm programmed into that cell if you need me for anything." He nodded to the table. "Good luck."

"*Shukran*," she murmured.

When the door latched behind him, it was all she could do not to do a happy dance in the middle of the room. She couldn't believe she was here! Her dream job. It had been offered so soon after she'd presented her doctoral thesis she could hardly believe it was real. It had taken her only two weeks to pack up her things in Chicago and find a quaint apartment here. Atef's assistant had emailed over some suggestions and she'd chosen the first one she'd seen. She'd been here a week already, getting everything unpacked and settling in. She would get to catalog, research, expand the history of the dead for the living, and act as a special consultant on the local dig sites up and down the Nile from September to April. Life could not get much better than this.

Elisa quickly typed a text to her best friend, Miriam, who was traveling who-knew-where these days.

> **Here. It's perfect. Xoxo**

Three dots appeared, disappeared, and reappeared.

> **You deserve it! Love and kisses from Dubai!**

Attached to the text was a selfie of Miriam, who appeared to be on the roof of a very tall building overlooking Dubai at sunset.

Living her best life, as always, Elisa thought as she slid her phone back into her pocket.

"Curses be damned," she said to the empty room.

The papers stacked neatly in front of her flew into the air and floated haphazardly to the floor. Elisa felt the hairs on the back of her neck stand up.

"How curious."

A few hours later, papers and notes were scattered on her preferred space, the floor, as she talked to herself to help her sort out this latest puzzle. All of the papers from the original dig and its itemized contents were in front of her. Thankfully, the previous Egyptologists managed to do a bit of their own documentation and exams so she didn't have to start completely from scratch.

Uncovered in 1881, this particular tomb and its inhabitant were a bit of a mystery. The tomb itself had been found in the Thebes necropolis. This had clearly been a person of some prominence, based on the type of mummification and his jewelry. Many distinguished funerary objects had been found with him. The list of cataloged items included a handful of shabti figures, four canopic jars, wine jugs, a small carved boat, and other ancient ephemera. The photographs of his tomb showed typical décor from the 18th dynasty's Book of the Dead: a few spells for navigating life successfully in the afterworld. What was important and noted at the time of the removal and initial investigation of the mummy in the 1880s was that the occupant's heart was missing. In its place, inside the chest, was a heart scarab.

Elisa got up and stretched. She shifted through the x-rays that had been taken in the months before her arrival. She couldn't help but notice the gold jewelry that flashed in front of her from the x-ray of the skull.

She wandered over to the mostly still-wrapped mummy and bent over to examine his face where the wrappings had fallen away with time.

"You had a nice square jaw, didn't you? You were probably very handsome."

She pulled her digital recorder from the pocket of her lab coat. "Based on dentition, and osteological features of the skull and pelvis, subject is male, approximately 30-40 years old, and 188 centimeters tall.

"There is no obvious indication of any physical trauma to the bones or skull and his teeth are all intact, leading me to believe he had access to good nutrition and diet."

Elisa glanced again at the bright indications of the X-rays and then at the neck of the mummy. "X-ray and visual inspection confirm the wearing of large earrings in both ears, in the Nubian style, and the presence of a king's collar in gold and gemstones around the neck."

"X-ray confirms the evisceration of the brain but the ocular nerves and surrounding tissue are intact, leading me to conclude that the mummification of this man was taken with care."

Elisa gently ran a finger over the top of his linen wrapping. "Ask Atef if we can get chemical analysis of the bitumen covering the wrapping. It's darker than most resins I've seen before and has taken on a black, shiny, almost lacquered appearance over time.

"All evidence points to the fact that this man came from wealth and status and was afforded all of the mummification rites and rituals of the 18th Dynasty, however, all mention of his name has been painstakingly removed from the lid of the sarcophagus. Check the shabti figures for additional carvings."

Elisa put the X-rays on a counter and bent to pick up a few photographs of the interior of the tomb. She frowned as she examined the black and white hieroglyphs: many of them depicted this person being forever damned in the afterlife.

Elisa chewed her bottom lip and then rubbed her blurry eyes. Why would someone go to such trouble to bury someone in such a prestigious way and then ensure their eternal damnation? She had only heard of two mummies being found without their hearts—King Tut himself and the venerated priest Ipi. The heart was the center of intelligence and emotion to the ancient Egyptians and the only way to be sure of navigating the afterlife successfully. There were thousands of images of Osiris or Anubis weighing the heart against the feather of truth at the entrance of the afterworld. If you had lived a good life, the heart would be lighter than the feather and you could pass on into the afterlife. If it weighed more than the feather, you were judged to have had an evil spirit in life and the crocodile-headed monster Ammit would immediately eat the heart.

It was hypothesized that Tut had had his heart removed accidentally during his hastily botched mummification, or that it had been damaged by an accident and was deemed unworthy to stay in his body. Ipi's heart had been found not long ago in a heap of natron bags used for mummification, seemingly mistaken for the bags that soak up liquids in the body and placed in a canopic jar in his tomb. To intentionally remove the heart, though, was one of the worst punishments Elisa could imagine for the soul of an ancient Egyptian.

Gaining a full understanding of who this man was was going to be a lot of work. It was a good thing she liked a challenge.

She studied the anthropoid sarcophagus. It was likely limestone with a wooden interior coffin and had, at one time, been brightly painted, but none of that remained now. It sat, ancient and worn, on a plinth in the middle of the room. She scanned the lid and ran her fingers gently over the deep chisel marks over where his name once was.

"Who did you piss off?" The painted eyes of the death mask that lay next to him held no answers, nor did the relatively well-preserved body in front of her.

On the table behind her, four canopic jars and a heart scarab were laid out. She picked up the scarab and turned it over. The inscribed stone was cold and heavy in her hand. The carved hieroglyphs on the back were so small she could barely read them. Elisa looked around for some kind of magnifying tool and found a large one on a stand with a light.

The fluorescent beam and glass made it much easier for her to read the script and she translated out loud:

Oh my heart of my love! Oh my heart of my love!
My heart of my different ages! Do not stand as a witness! Do not oppose me in
the tribunal!
Do not show your hostility against me before the Keeper of the Balance!
For you are my ka which is in my body, the protector who causes my limbs to
be healthy! Go forth for yourself to the good place to which we hasten!
Do not cause our name to stink to the entourage who make men in heaps!
What is good for us is good for the judge! May the heart stretch at the verdict!
Do not
speak lies in the presence of god! Behold
You are distinguished, existing as a justified one!
It is indeed well that you should hear.

"Well, that was spectacularly unhelpful," Elisa sighed and returned the scarab to the table. She'd need to write down that translation while it was still fresh. She turned to the binder on the table at the front of the room and began recording what she'd just read. She'd include measurements and specifics later.

Halfway through her record-keeping, she felt a sudden presence. She started to stand up and then shook her head. She would know if someone walked in—the metal door was too loud to be ignored. But then a low voice came from somewhere behind her.

"That was well done. Most people don't get it on the first try."

Elisa dropped the pen she was holding and turned around slowly. In front of her was one of the most beautiful men she had ever seen. His dark eyes matched the darkness of his hair, and he was dressed in the style of the ancient Egyptians—a linen kilt with metal arm bands and a collar where she could clearly make out lapis, carnelian, and amethyst. She glanced at the body of the mummy and then at the figure in front of her. Even in death, the features were unmistakable.

Elisa felt her heart racing and her mouth go dry. All of the blood drained from her face and left a cold tingling behind.

It was jet lag. Had she eaten today? Maybe she'd fallen asleep while she was reading. She'd always had an overactive imagination.

Her mouth moved, but no sound came out. The figure in front of her watched all of this without comment but suddenly he smiled. "Hello."

And Dr. Elisa Kent fainted for the first time in her life.

Chapter Two

The cold, hard floor under Elisa smelled like bleach. She opened her eyes as her head pounded and saw two of the most perfect feet she'd ever seen. They were bare with long toes, high arches, and attached to muscular legs. As her eyes crept up this man's body, she realized he was vaguely hazy but beautiful. Maybe she'd hit her head harder than she thought. Concussions could cause vision issues, right?

His arms were crossed, and his brow furrowed while he stared down at her. He did not look particularly impressed, though he certainly was impressive.

Elisa got to her feet, slowly, with one hand holding her head. Science and logic defied everything that had happened in the last several minutes. A thousand and one questions battled for attention, but all she could think to do was introduce herself.

"I'm—"

"I know who you are. I knew your great-grandfather. You look very like him, Dr. Kent."

Despite this man's ancient garments, he spoke like a cultured British aristocrat.

"I think maybe I'm having a stroke." Elisa needed to sit down. Her head was swimming with pain and confusion. She moved to the closest chair and leaned forward with her head in her hands. While she was trying to remember where the nearest hospital was to go get herself a CT ASAP, the man spoke again.

"You know, I was worried when I heard a woman was coming to do this job, but you're handling this better than your predecessors."

She lifted one hand slowly away from her face and looked at him through her hair.

"So you're the curse."

The eyebrows stayed furrowed, but a small smirk played around the edges of his mouth. "Oh, no. I'm not *the* curse. I *am* cursed. I'm hoping you might be able to help me with that."

Elisa again found herself speechless. She blinked at him a few times before what he'd said registered.

"I'm sorry, what? I don't even know who you are."

"That is easily remedied. You may call me Nef." He bowed slightly to her as he introduced himself. The collar at his neck shifted and she could swear it almost rattled as he moved.

"This isn't possible. I mean, you're a what? A ghost? This is a joke, right? Atef is playing a joke on me since it's my first day here?" She looked around. "Very funny, Atef. You can come out now." Nothing happened. Nef continued to stare down his very straight nose at her.

"Right. Well, I'm going to go to the hospital and get myself checked out for a concussion, stroke, aneurysm, poisoning, and anything else I can think of, and you…well…" Elisa looked him up and down as she stood. "Won't be here when I get back since you're a hallucination or something, so nice to meet you."

Her bag was on the table near her, and she grabbed it and walked toward the door.

"Thutmos."

Elisa stopped and looked at him, "Excuse me?"

"You asked who I 'pissed off.' It was Thutmose III. The greatest pharaoh in all of Egypt."

Elisa scoffed, "I mean, that's arguable. Many people would make a case for Rams—"

The look on his face hadn't changed as she'd turned to argue with him, but the brows had deepened even further if that were possible. "You're serious, aren't you? Not about the greatest pharaoh bit, but about pissing off Thutmos?"

"Indeed. I may be many things, but a liar I am not."

A hysterical laugh started to escape her, and Elisa barely contained it. "I don't understand any of this."

The furrow lessened a bit, and the smirk was back along with an imperious eyebrow raise. "You are a woman of knowledge. I understand. Would you like to know?"

Elisa had a momentary internal struggle between her rational mind and her curiosity. Curiosity won. She nodded.

"Please," he gestured to the chair she'd been sitting in.

What could it hurt to indulge this fantasy for a few minutes? Or hallucination? Either way, she could still go to the hospital, unless she really was having a stroke and then she'd be dead before it mattered. She set her bag down again, shook her hair behind her, and looked at the man standing before her. An involuntary chill ran up her arms as he peered down at her.

"Do I scare you?"

"I'm not sure. Maybe. Intimidate might be the better word."

"Is this better?" In the blink of an eye, his linen kilt had been replaced by a blue button-down shirt, a suit coat, grey slacks, and dress shoes. His shoulder-length hair was now bound back at the nape of his neck and his goatee was perfectly trimmed. It was very similar to what Atef had had on when he met her this morning, though the shades of the fabric were darker and more expensive looking on Nef and the cut was better. He looked even more exquisite somehow.

Elisa gaped again. "How did you do that?"

"We'll get to that." Nef leaned on the table across from her and re-folded his arms across his chest. The fabric at his arms pulled with his movement.

This is the most elaborate hallucination of all time, Elisa thought.

"I won't start with 'Once upon a time,' though I know that's a common phrase for stories like this." He cleared his throat and seemed to relax a little.

"I was born in what you call 1487 BCE in the great city of Thebes. My father was vizier to Hatshepsut, and it was expected that I would follow the same path. I was raised with Thutmos, though I was many years younger than he. We were as brothers." He pushed off from the table and started pacing the length between the tables. His feet didn't make a sound on the tiled floor.

"It pains me to remember those days now. Days where we ran together on the banks of the Nile, played *senet* together, raced chariots, and waited for him to take the throne until his stepmother renounced it or died. While we waited, we lived. We traveled. I was his constant companion until one day he sent me on an errand. I was advisor to the future king. It was my duty to determine the status of our enemies and our allies to the north and south. He needed to know what might happen if he took back the throne by force. Would our allies remain our allies? Some of them would, but some would not. I tried...what's your word?" He scratched his chin. "Ah, yes. Diplomacy. I found talking more successful than killing, but I was good at both."

Nef paused for a moment to look at Elisa. She could suddenly imagine him with a sword or spear and the terrifying figure he might have been in battle. She shrank back in her chair a bit.

"I was fifteen when Thutmos sent me to do his bidding and assure his allegiances on the throne. Still a boy by your standards, but then, I was a man worthy of the respect my name carried. Neferamun."

Elisa's mind whirled. She had never come across that name being related to anyone in the 18th dynasty, certainly not as a vizier. If that were true, he would have been considered almost a prince.

"I returned eight years later. When I left him, Thutmos had married and started a family. He had no more power than I did at the time. When I returned, he was pharaoh. Hatshepsut died and all the years of my traveling bore fruit. The wise men I'd spoken to remained loyal to Thutmos and we had peace, for a time." He paused, thoughtfully, and rubbed his forefinger and thumb together.

"Do you know of the feast of the lotus?"

Elisa had been so lost in his story that she didn't realize he'd asked the question of her. "Uh, I'm familiar with it. It's a myth. But what does that have to do with you?"

Both eyebrows went up this time. "No, not a myth. It was very real, and, I believe it led to my death. Once a year, we gathered together to celebrate our great fortune. We would place candles in a sculpture of a lotus, place them in the Nile, and make a wish. If the lotus stayed afloat, the wish would be granted.

"On the year I returned, we had our usual feast. We were celebrating. I was happy to be home finally. Thutmose was happy to welcome me back as his brother and adviser. As the sun set, we gathered our candles and then I saw her." He seemed lost to his memories because the face that had been hard and stoic since he'd appeared suddenly went soft with love or longing.

"She was the most beautiful woman I had ever laid eyes on. I didn't know who she was, but we looked at each other and walked to the edge of the Nile together. We placed our candles in the river. I wished for her. To start a family. Both of our candles floated away."

"I saw her again a few days later and asked her name. Renena, she told me. She cried to me and told me how unhappy she was that she was going to be married to someone she didn't love. I fell in love with her. I tried to save her. I told Thutmos about her, asked him to intervene. I told him how much I loved her. He wished me joy but wouldn't bother helping. I couldn't run away with her and leave my duties or the responsibility to my pharaoh, but I knew enough people along the river to help get her out of the city, at least for a while. Long enough for her marriage to be dissolved. We made a plan and executed it."

"The following day, all of Thebes was chaos. Pharaoh's sister, Neferure, was missing."

"Well shit."

"Don't interrupt." He said sternly but then softened. "But, exactly. Shit." He took a deep breath and closed his eyes. "I couldn't have known. She was no more than a child when I left. As soon as I realized my error, I confessed to Thutmos. He was furious, but he seemed to understand. Neferure was his half-sister and loyal to her mother, Hatshepsut. She had been a thorn in his side since he'd taken his rightful place as pharaoh. He actually laughed when I went to him and told him my tale. He forgave me and I told his general where she could be found.

"It took them a long time to find her. Too long. We were on the brink of war with Assyria and some of those who had been loyal to Hatshepsut were not happy when they found out the vizier had spirited away her daughter. Thutmos began blaming me. As our enemies grew, so did his anger. He said I should have known better than to love her."

THE FEAST OF THE LOTUS

"He left to fight the war in Assyria with his general. I stayed behind to be keeper of Thebes. Though his anger raged, he still trusted me to be the keeper of our people while he was away. Or so I thought." Nef looked down at his hands as he rubbed them together and then slid them in his pockets. His voice was quiet as he finished his tale.

"One night…I drank my usual glass of wine and felt…strange. When I awoke, I was in an unfamiliar place looking up at a man standing over that." He gestured absentmindedly to the sarcophagus.

Nef started pacing again. "I was afraid. I didn't know what was happening. I panicked. Gradually, I started to understand. I had been cursed. Thutmoses' fury was hidden from me. He must have felt I had betrayed him with Neferure, with our southern enemies. He wanted to make sure I would be damned. The people of Thebes loved me, so he gave me a funeral befitting my station but then cursed me to damnation by removing my name, *my name* from everything. Stealing my heart from my body."

Elisa saw the veins in his neck start to show with this last sentence, but also the sadness that crept into his transparent features. He clenched his fists and then opened his hands helplessly.

"Whatever I did to him was nothing compared to what he did to me in death."

If he had been alive, Elisa would have thought his body would be seething in quiet desperation. She couldn't imagine what it was to have your whole identity as a person stolen from you because of a perceived slight. She'd known other pharaohs to do worse with less though. Or so the glyphs and scribes said.

Elisa knew she shouldn't speak yet, so she kept her thoughts to herself.

"It was 1886 when my tomb was opened and in 1903, I met your great-grandfather at the British Museum. He was the first to attempt to translate that scarab you found. For some reason, that he could never understand, the reading of it aloud makes me visible to the reader only. I enjoyed his company for the years he was there. I watched the World Wars from London, heard about Hitler scattering my family all over the world. I listened. I learned. After he retired, he would still come and visit me on occasion. After he passed, I got packed up and shipped back to Cairo where I've waited. My remains have been here for many years. Now, by some twist of fate or design, they're in your hands."

Chapter Three

Overwhelmed. Elisa had no idea what to do with all the information he'd just dumped in her lap. She had listened, captivated by what he'd told her, but unsure whether or not to believe half of what he'd said. She needed to process all of this information, and she didn't even know where to begin.

Just as she started to ask a question, there was a knock on the door and then it opened. Atef peeked his head in. He took in the room, the papers on the floor, and Elisa sitting in a chair. She wondered if she looked as bewildered as she felt.

"I just wanted to see how you were getting on. Digging right in from the looks of things."

She chanced a look at Nef, but he was leaning on the table across from her. Atef hadn't looked at him at all. She got up and moved toward him to try to draw Atef's attention to the other figure in the room, but he didn't seem to notice anything.

"It's going well. Thanks."

"Would you like to join me upstairs for lunch? I can also show you to your office if you'd like."

Perfect. An escape and a chance to think through all of what she'd just heard.

"I'd love to, actually. Let me just clean all this up."

"You can leave it if you'd like. No one will disturb it."

She smiled warmly at him. Even if she'd wanted to say something to this…ghost, she wouldn't have known what to say. *Thanks for the info. Enjoy your shitty afterlife. I'm catching the first plane back to the States.*

When she looked back at Nef before leaving, his face was the same it had been—his brow was furrowed and his arms were crossed, but sadness had crept into his features to replace the sternness she'd seen most of the morning.

She made polite conversation with Atef as they made their way into the offices upstairs. He bought her a coffee in the café and after taking a few restoratives sips her mind cleared a little.

"Atef, I know there are situations where a successive pharaoh has tried to remove identifying information on tombs and monuments of previous pharaohs. Do you know if that's ever happened outside of the pharaonic line?"

He stirred his tea and thought for a moment. "I'm sure there have been cases. Pharaohs are notorious for being...drama queens, you know? If someone betrayed them in life, it was the ultimate punishment to ruin their plans for the afterlife. Do you think that's what happened here?"

"I think it's a very good possibility. The inscription of this...man's name was chiseled off the front of the sarcophagus and the canopic jars."

"You know," he sipped his tea and shook a finger at her, "the Egyptians did like to recycle. We've found several cases where someone would die suddenly, without having prepared their burial chamber and the priests just used funerary ephemera that was intended for someone else."

"I think that's a less likely case here, though. Mostly because in the instances that I've read about, they still inscribe the tomb, the items, with a name."

He nodded in agreement. "That is true. The deceased's name was just as important a feature as anything to ensure a happy afterlife. Just as important as the *ba, ka,* the heart, the shadow, and the *akh.*" He paused at a doorway. Elisa hadn't been paying any attention and had no idea how they'd gotten here. She was going to need a map.

"Here we are." The door opened and Elisa walked into a beautiful room that felt a little out of place in the rest of the museum. The walls were dark and already the shelves were lined with books. A beautiful carpet was spread on the floor over marbled tiles. A large desk was positioned in the back of the room, in front of a huge window. Almost the entire back wall was glass. The view beyond the window took her breath away. Framed perfectly in the background were the three most famous pyramids in the world. She would never get over the awe she felt every time she saw them.

"Will this do?"

"It's beautiful, Atef. I may never leave."

Atef chuckled. "That is my hope. I'm just down the hall if you need anything."

"Actually, I was wondering if we could run the mass spec on a section of the wrappings. The bitumen is darker and more lacquered than I've encountered before."

Atef raised his eyebrows and then smiled. "Of course. Whatever you need." He turned to leave, then stopped in the doorway. "I'm glad it went well downstairs. I was half afraid you'd run screaming from the building after half an hour. But then you're a Kent. I hear you don't scare easily."

Elisa wasn't sure how to take this comment but smiled back, "Just another day at the office."

Three hours later, Elisa's neck ached. She still hadn't found anything in any database on Neferamun. He simply didn't exist in the historical record. Not on anything that had been digitized anyway. Thanks to Thutmos' scribe she knew almost everything there was to know about the pharaoh and his longer-than-average reign, but nothing about Nef. She had, unfortunately, confirmed everything else he'd told her, at least as much as she could. There were still some gaps, but not as many as she had hoped there might be. She had even found historical references to Neferure being kidnapped but nothing said by whom.

Elisa stood up and stretched. She glanced at the copious notes she'd taken and then turned to the window. Everything she wanted was here. The history, the questions that needed to be answered, the mummies needing names, the promise of being remembered for eternity. She couldn't deny that she found that last notion more than a little romantic.

The legacy her great-grandfather started all those years ago was something undeniable. Most people knew the name Howard Carter. They remembered him as the man who had found King Tutankhamen's tomb. They often forgot that it had taken him five years to find it or that there were other Egyptologists on the same journey he was on. Her great-grandfather, Charles Kent, had been one of them. He'd fallen in love with Egypt the moment he set foot on her shores. He spent more than a decade here and then became curator for the British Museum long after.

She couldn't help but think of him now, and the connection that they shared to the body in the lab. She wondered idly what he would have done in this situation, and then inspiration struck her.

Elisa picked up her phone and chose one of the few numbers on her speed dial. Her aunt picked up on the second ring.

"Darling! I've been emailing. You were supposed to call me after you got in the GEM today."

Guilt flashed through her. "I know, Mae. I'm sorry. It's been…busy."

"Is it wonderful and amazing?"

"It's everything I hoped for and more. I'll send you a picture of the view from my office window. It looks right over the pyramids."

"Oh, that's wonderful. I'm so jealous. I remember the first time I saw them in 1960. Maybe if I ever get off this bloody oxygen tank, I can come for a visit." She coughed for good measure.

Elisa stifled a sigh. This was a recurring conversation. If she didn't steer her somewhere else soon, she'd be hearing a list of all of her aunt's ailments.

"Mae. I was wondering if you still have Charles Kent's old journals lying around somewhere."

"Oh, love, I'm sure I do. You know I never throw anything out. But what do you need with those old things?"

Elisa could picture the room they were probably in. Mae's big old house, Berkyn Manor, in Slough might well have been a museum itself. She'd kept nearly everything that had belonged to her grandfather, father, and brother—Elisa's father—as well as her own collection from the digs she'd been on.

"It turns out I'm working on a project that great grandad also worked on in 1903. I was hoping there might be something in there that might help me work through some of this. It's an unidentified mummy from Thebes."

"Ah! Nef, is it?"

Elisa almost dropped the phone. "What did you say?"

"Nef. That was the nickname he gave to the only unidentified mummy granddad ever worked on. I remember. When he'd gotten senile, he wouldn't stop talking about the ghost he knew. I read his journals in the seventies after he died and there were pages and pages of notes about him. I thought he'd gone stark raving mad myself."

"Really?"

"Just so. I think I know the exact cabinet they're in. I'll have Theo take a look and send them to you, shall I?"

"Yes. That would be great. I'll email you the address here."

"Wonderful. I wish I could bring them to you myself, but my arthritis has been acting up again and I hate to travel when it's cold. Damned English weather. I'm sure it's much nicer where you are."

"It is. Not a hint of a chill even though it's February. Thank you for sending those over."

"Of course, my pet. You know, if you end up needing it, I have a friend who is a damn good psychic. She could do a séance for you. Or Father Decker would happily come over and do an exorcism."

Elisa couldn't imagine Father Decker traveling anywhere at his age. He must have been almost ninety by now.

"I'll keep that in mind."

"All right. Don't do anything I wouldn't do! Find yourself a handsome Egyptian and have some babies for me before I die, would you?"

This time Elisa did sigh, audibly. "Yes, Aunt. Better run. I'll call again soon."

"Kisses, darling!"

As soon as she ended the call, she opened the often-ignored-email on her phone and saw the ten or so missed emails from her aunt. All from this morning. She replied with the address to the most recent one and marked all the others as "read."

"Checking up on me?"

The voice came from behind her again and she turned so quickly, she banged her hip on the corner of her desk.

"Ouch." She rubbed at her offended hip and murmured, "That'll be a bruise."

Elisa glanced up and saw for the second time the specter she'd met that morning. He looked entirely at ease sitting on the leather sofa on the opposite side of the room. His arms were resting on the back, and he had one ankle resting on the opposite knee. He looked much more like a twentieth-century billionaire than an 18th Dynasty Egyptian ghost. Amusement played around his eyes and mouth, directed at her, most likely.

"You really can't keep startling me like this. I've already given myself a concussion and now a bad hip because of you."

"Perhaps you should learn to be more aware of your surroundings."

"My surroundings have nothing to do with a thirty-five-hundred-year-old ghost choosing to spook me every chance he gets." She walked around the front of her desk and leaned against it, arms folded.

"And yes, I was checking up on you. But you must be doing the same, because why else are you here?" She tried to be stern.

"I thought you might have some questions for me after you had some time to think about what I told you this morning."

"Actually, I do." She reached behind her to pick up the notepad where she'd been taking notes and flipped to a page of questions she'd written down in case she ever decided to go back down to the lab. She scanned them briefly then looked at him. This time her eyebrows rose.

"Wait. How did you know I was here?"

He half-smiled. It disarmed her a little. "Call it a...hunch."

Hmmm. He wasn't telling her something. She looked at her questions again. Where to even begin?

"First, you said you woke up in 1903. So you have no idea what happened between your death and that date."

"I was awakened in 1903, yes. And no. I don't. I didn't dream. Didn't seem to exist. I was there, and then I was...here."

"You said you listened and learned, but to what and whom? How is your English so good?"

"Your great-grandfather. It took me a while to figure out what was happening. What I could and couldn't do. When I first met Charles Kent, we couldn't communicate at all. No one has spoken ancient Egyptian in thousands of years. He eventually told me it didn't sound like anything else he'd ever heard. He drew symbols and I caught on. I've picked up Arabic out of necessity, and French over the years, too. Languages I know you speak as well."

She had been jotting down more notes as he spoke, but at that she looked up, startled.

"How did you know that?"

"I Googled you."

How was that even possible? She thought he might elaborate but when he didn't, she asked the obvious question. "How?"

"I can do some things in the physical realm. It's quite exhausting, but I can move a mouse and type on a keyboard if I have the inclination."

"But there's no computer in the lab other than the laptop Atef gave me this morning."

"It doesn't have to be in the lab. I seem to be able to go anywhere in this building, just as I stalked the halls of the British Museum. I just can't be too far from my body. The farther I go, the weaker I become."

"Interesting." She was writing furiously now. "So *you* moved the papers this morning?"

He looked sheepish but still stern. "I was trying to get your attention."

"You did."

"Did I? You seemed to ignore me. I had a few other tricks up my sleeve, but you found what you needed to find without much help from me. Much faster than the others."

"Did you scare them off intentionally?"

"Yes and no."

More that he wasn't telling her.

"What is it that you want from me? Why me?"

"You're the expert, right? Now that you know who I am, you'll find the scroll I need and my heart so I can leave this place and go where I belong. To the Afterworld. Back to Neferure."

"Even after she lied to you?"

He frowned again. "Not that it's any of your concern, but I've had quite a long time to forgive her."

"Look, that's great and all," Elisa set the notebook down on the desk again. "But this is completely illogical. I have no idea how I'm supposed to find the missing pieces you're looking for. Your name has been removed from everything. There's no historical record of you ever existing. There's no archeological record of you ever existing anywhere other than where you are. If your heart and scroll weren't in the tomb with you, then I don't even know where to begin looking." She turned to sit behind her desk.

"Not to mention, I have an actual job to do. I don't think Atef would be very happy to have hired me and then I go off on some fool's errand that I can't even tell him about, because, again, you don't exist. I can't just run down to his office and tell him I know who the mummy belongs to, met you, and am therefore done with my research. There's simply no evidence."

"But Dr. Kent, I *do* have some ideas on where you might look for my heart and the scroll."

"Where?"

"In Thebes, of course. The Valley of Kings."

A headache was starting to form behind her eyes. She pinched the bridge of her nose and tried to stave it off. "My answer is no. I need to make a good impression here. It's my reputation on the line. The last thing I need is people thinking I'm crazy and talking to someone no one else can see or hear. If that got out, I wouldn't be able to help you at all."

"I'll bear that in mind." And with that, he was gone.

Chapter Four

Elisa finally packed her bag and left for the day around seven. Atef had come to check on her before he left and seemed surprised she was still there. She was a little surprised herself. She'd been so caught up in looking for more information that she'd lost track of time.

When she finally got back to her apartment, her brain was full and she was mentally exhausted. She wanted to curl up with fast food and her favorite horrible reality TV show and forget most of what had happened that day. Unfortunately, Egypt didn't have any Southern fried chicken sandwiches yet, and the only trash TV she could find was all in Arabic. Her brain was too tired to do the work of translation, so she settled for curling up on her sofa and staring at the boxes still piled in her living room while she ate a microwave dinner.

Eventually, she'd have to finish unpacking. Most of what was left in the boxes were books. She had very few material possessions that she'd deemed important enough to take with her. Her books, though, were something that she could never leave behind, despite having cost a fortune to ship.

The apartment was large by Cairo standards, with two bedrooms, two baths, a living room, dining room, kitchen, and balcony that overlooked the Nile. It came furnished, which she was grateful for because she didn't have any furniture worth hauling to another country and wasn't interested in shopping for any. It was comfortable and modern. Vastly different from the museum-mansion she'd grown up in with Aunt Mae.

Elisa had never stayed in any place long enough to make it a home until she'd been forced to move in with her aunt after her parents died. She had bounced around with them from dig sites and university housing until she was sixteen. Her homeschooling with them enabled her to learn whatever she wanted, and by the time she became a teenager, she dreamed about rebelling against any and everything having to do with Egypt. Once, she had enjoyed all of the trivia and been proud of the fact that she'd memorized the chronology of the pharaohs from the Old and New kingdoms by the time she was five—mostly because her parents had been so proud—but it eventually became boring. Though she figured that at a certain point, pretty much everything got boring to teenage girls.

She had asked to stay at the dig house and not to be dragged to yet another "exciting find" in a new tomb in Thebes. The diggers had just cleared a secret tomb that was small and cramped. Both of her parents had gone in to explore when the whole tomb collapsed on top of both of them, burying them in rubble. It had taken everyone on site hours to dig them out and by the time they had, they were both dead. Her mother had suffered a punctured lung and her father had had his skull crushed.

When the knock at the door came, she'd been watching dubbed MTV as loud as their television would go and almost didn't hear it. It was common to have someone from the dig come and tell her that her parents were running late because cell phone service at the time was virtually non-existent in the middle of the desert. She was not expecting to open the door and find Egyptian police and their dig site manager with news that would alter her life forever.

Elisa remembered falling to the ground in shock after they told her the news. It was as though her whole world collapsed on top of her, too. Years later, she'd gotten a copy of the Egyptian autopsy reports and had read them enough to have memorized them.

A few days later, Aunt Mae had come to collect her and her parents' remains to be interred at the family mausoleum in England. Because of her homeschooling, she was technically finished with school, her parents only had to submit the paperwork for her to get her diploma, but they hadn't yet. Aunt Mae had taken care of that, which had given her the time she needed to grieve. She'd wandered the halls of the estate for months, looking out the windows and feeling numb to everything.

She'd been mad at the world. Mad at Egypt and everything it had taken from her. Worst of all, there were so many artifacts in

Mae's home that reminded her of her parents. The first few months there, she barely left her room, but one day she got so angry, she almost set fire to a death mask in the study and all it represented.

Her cousin Theo had come home at Christmas break from Oxford. He didn't directly engage her at first, they didn't know each other that well. But after a few days, he'd started to leave books he thought she might like in front of her door. It started with Keats, then Browning, and eventually Christina Rosetti. About as far from ancient Egypt as she could imagine.

She wanted to talk about what she was reading, she had to, with someone. After mass on Christmas Eve, she shyly engaged him in conversation about "Goblin Market." The Romantics made death and love sound so...romantic. The macabre was celebrated. Her grief eased.

Theo encouraged her ideas and then suggested she get a place at Oxford in the fall. She was smart enough. Aunt Mae had been over the moon when Elisa said she wanted to go to university. Elisa's inheritance would have seen her through many years of wandering around the giant house doing absolutely nothing, but she couldn't stand to just sit and do nothing anymore. Her parents had instilled a love of exploration and learning in her and she wasn't going to waste that gift. She wanted to make them proud.

She hoped she had. Her expensive education had taken her all around the world. She'd started out in English, but history and eventually Egyptology had called to her. It was in her blood, after all.

It might have hurt her to come back to the place where they'd died, but somehow, it made her feel closer to them. She was continuing the work they had begun. She walked over to one of the few framed photographs that had come with her from her latest temporary place in Chicago. She picked it up and held the cold silver frame in her hands. Her mother looked adoringly at her father. His arm was wrapped around her and he smiled enthusiastically at the camera. They had their standard dig clothes on and sweated in the Egyptian heat, but they couldn't have been happier. Elisa, a much younger version, stood in between them, showing a gaping hole in her smile where her front teeth were missing.

Crash.

The noise behind her startled her out of her memories.

Thud. Thud.

The noises were coming from the second bedroom that she'd intended to turn into a home office and library. Looking around for a weapon of some kind, she went to the kitchen and found the heaviest thing she could find: a cast iron skillet.

Elisa tip-toed toward the bedroom, wondering how someone could have gotten into the apartment. It was three floors up.

The room was dark with everything thrown in shadow from the streetlights glowing an odd orange outside. Elisa felt silently for the light switch, flicked it on, and jumped screaming into the room brandishing the skillet above her head.

A cat blinked at her from one of the tops of the boxes.

Elisa leaned against the door jamb and tried to get her heart to stop pounding. She could feel the adrenaline pumping through her, but the intruder calmly started licking its paw.

"Not that intimidating, I guess."

She walked over to the dark grey cat with black spots. It looked like a miniature leopard that had had kohl eyeliner put on it. It didn't move as she slowly approached but seemed to regard her with an almost royal disinterest. Elisa put a hand out to try to pet it and the cat nudged its nose immediately into her hand.

"Well, hello there. Where did you come from?"

The cat purred in response and turned itself to allow Elisa's hand to run along its back. She looked over and realized that the window in the room was half open. She vaguely remembered opening it the night before to let the cool breeze off the Nile come in when she'd been unpacking.

"I imagine you're looking for food, but I don't have any."

She remembered the half-eaten frozen dinner in the living room and wondered if the cat might take any interest in that. She retrieved it and set it on the box next to the cat who sniffed it and lapped up the last of the sauce there.

Satisfied, she decided to leave the window open in case the cat wanted to go back to wherever it had come from.

"Right. I'm off to bed. Long day. Goodnight."

She turned the light off and rolled her eyes at herself. *Great. Now I'm talking to cats. I really should get out more.*

But getting out meant people and getting close to people inevitably meant that they left you at some point, so she wouldn't allow herself that comfort.

Cats it is, she thought as she brushed her teeth. She washed her face, changed into her nightgown, and snuggled into the down comforter. She drifted off thinking about her smiling parents.

The next morning, she woke up to find the cat curled into her stomach, asleep and purring. Elisa scratched it behind the ears, and it yawned at her.

"I guess if you're staying, we'll have to think of a name for you."

It got up, stretched, and licked her on the nose.

Elisa laughed at the sandpaper of its tongue.

"How about Bastet?"

It licked her on the forehead at this and she considered that all of the approval she was going to get. There were worse things to be named after than the Egyptian goddess of cats, after all.

"I'll pick up some food for you on the way home if you're still here."

She got up and stretched, too. "Today, though, I've got a long day of cataloging ahead of me and a ghost to ignore."

Her shower was quick and she dressed in her usual "office" attire: a button-down shirt, khaki slacks, and sensible black flats. Her long auburn hair found its usual place in a bun at the nape of her neck. She checked her reflection as she applied a small bit of mascara and light lip gloss. Her freckled cheeks and her mother's bright green eyes stared back at her. She smoothed the shirt over her curves and walked out the door.

On her ride in the cab to the GEM, she went through a mental checklist of everything she wanted to try to get accomplished today. Her goal was to start small with the smaller artifacts from the tomb then work her way up the sarcophagus and then his mummy. She wouldn't let the hunt for his mythical heart or the supposed scroll divert her from the fact that she had an actual job to do. If she had some spare time, she might poke around a bit, but for scientific reasons only. She was not going to let her reputation as one of the foremost experts on unidentified mummies and one of the youngest Egyptologists in her field slide. She would make her parents and her great-grandfather proud one way or another.

It took her longer than she would have liked to remember the key code for the door. She was a firm believer that if she didn't write it down, it didn't exist, and she'd forgotten to jot it on her notepad after Atef let her.

When she finally did remember the code, she opened the door to a quiet, empty lab. She'd steeled herself for another confrontation, but there was no sign of Nef, at least none that she could see. She went to the closet, hung up her sweater and purse, and retrieved a lab coat and gloves. The first task was the heart scarab. It needed to be examined, x-rayed, photographed, and cataloged properly. Elisa retrieved it from its box and started going through the routine she was so comfortable with. She'd been helping her parents with tasks like this since she was old enough to be considered responsible with them.

Half an hour later, she heard a throat clearing behind her. She jerked a little but was less startled than the last two times he'd surprised her. No one else could have come into the room as soundlessly, so she instantly knew who the noise belonged to.

She ignored him.

The throat cleared again.

She didn't look up from her transcription. "I was wondering when you'd appear today."

"I'm surprised you came back."

"I told you. I have a job to do."

"You did. And the prospect of having a ghost around wasn't going to deter you?"

Elisa did look up and turned to him now. He was wearing a white button-down with the sleeves rolled up to the elbow and khaki slacks. His hair was loose around his shoulders and fell in ebony waves. She chuckled at his choice of footwear today. He wore white Chuck Taylor's.

"Not even a bossy one. I don't scare that easily."

Elisa pushed away from her table, scarab in hand, and set it aside. She got the next item on her list, one of four small canopic jars, and started taking measurements.

"And what about what I've asked of you? Will you look?"

"I think I answered that question yesterday. The chances that your lost items are still in the Valley of Kings are more than slim. It's more likely they've been removed and are somewhere in this building or have been shipped off to a collection in another museum somewhere. Especially if they weren't marked. Which we know they weren't."

His ever-present scowl deepened. "And you don't think it's at least worth going?"

"No. I don't feel like traipsing all over Egypt on a wild goose chase right now." She turned back to her binder. "Besides, I'd need permission to go to the dig sites and I have to tell them why I'm going and where."

Nef shifted closer to her and leaned against the desk she was working on. He grumbled and crossed his arms in what she was starting to consider his signature pose.

"What if I could tell you where?"

Elisa stopped, intrigued. Nef noticed her pause and took advantage.

"That's where I was this morning. I went a few labs over to have a look at where they're keeping Thutmos. What's left of him anyway. Then I went to look at the things of his that are on display in the museum. A few things are missing. I think I know where they are."

Entranced, Elisa raised a questioning eyebrow and finally looked at him.

"Well...where?"

"You know it was the custom of pharaohs to start building their tombs long before they died, yes?"

Irritated, she gestured for him to continue.

"Thutmos was aware of grave robbers. Not only did we have them in our time, but it was common for priests and pharaohs even to go into other tombs and remove any riches they thought they might be able to use to benefit the wealth of Egypt. How do you think Hatshepsut paid for her massive temple at Luxor?"

Elisa's mouth gaped open at him. It had never occurred to her to get first-hand information from him before. She was too busy being overwhelmed by her new job and the fact that a ghost was following her. A ghost that wanted to send her on an impossible errand.

She remembered to close her mouth as he continued.

"Thutmos wanted to hide whatever wealth he could and other objects that might be necessary in the afterlife. So, he built a second compartment, a hidden one, in his tomb."

He watched her as this information sunk in. "As his vizier, I knew all about it. I even helped him plan where it should be. I didn't see any of the objects we discussed amongst his belongings, which leads me to believe…"

"They're still there," Elisa finished for him.

She turned back to the jar, no longer feeling the cool clay beneath her gloved fingers. The thought of what a discovery like this could mean for her sunk in followed by the reality of how idiotic she would sound going to Atef and asking for permission to scour a tomb that had already been scoured to within an inch of its life for remaining artifacts. What would she tell him? She had a hunch? She had no evidence that anything like this existed. Nothing in the text, nothing in anything she was cataloging. Just the word of a 3,500-year-old ghost that she happened to be on speaking terms with.

She sighed, regretfully. "It's not enough. I can't just go in with no proof—"

Nef made a sound like a growl and pushed away from the table. "You and your proof. Your *evidence*. Why is my word not enough? Why can you not just believe me?"

"As much as I'd like to, I have to be able to tell them what I'm looking for. Not just my boss, but the Egyptian government. They're very proud of everything that's in those tombs. Even if they did let me in with no real reason, they send inspectors to look at every single object that comes out. I'd never just be allowed to walk away with whatever Thutmos kept in there and bring it back here."

"Then we'll just have to sneak in."

"We? I–"

Elisa was cut off by whatever she was going to say next when the click of the lock on the door sounded.

Atef walked in, a concerned smile on his face.

"Ah, Elisa! Am I interrupting?" Atef looked around at the empty room. "It sounded like you were talking to someone."

She got up and smiled back trying to keep the embarrassment at bay. "Oh, no. I just talk to myself sometimes when I'm working on something."

He nodded though he looked like he didn't quite believe her. He stood in front of the door to let someone else into the room.

"Elisa, may I introduce Robert Grant? He's working on his internship with us this spring and I thought you might like an extra pair of hands to help you catalog, especially since you got off to such a good start yesterday. He's especially well-versed in chemical analysis, so I thought he might help you with those wrappings."

Robert was about as tall as Atef, but he was about as pale as the white walls. Elisa assumed he spent more time in fluorescent lab lighting than he did in the sun. His mop of brown hair could have used a cut, and he looked as excited to be in here as a puppy about to have his first bath. Despite that, he stuck his hand out politely and shook hers. "Hi. Nice to meet you."

"An American? Nice to meet you, too."

Robert almost smiled. "And you're a Brit."

Elisa shrugged. "From all over, really, but my family is British, yes."

"Robert has been working in other areas of the museum for the last month, so he's well acquainted with our SOPs." Atef ushered Robert more fully into the room.

"Excellent. Well, I've really just started. I'm sure you'll be a big help."

Atef put his hands in his pockets, seeming pleased with the decision to bring Robert in. "I'll leave you two to it then. Let me know if you need anything."

Atef left them alone and Robert eyed the room as if he were expecting something to jump out at him at any moment.

Elisa tried to get his attention as he moved to the closet to put on a lab coat. "Are you all right?"

Robert flushed and waved her off. "Oh, yeah. Fine. It's just that this room has an um...reputation with the interns."

"Is that right?"

He nodded as he slid the coat on and found a pair of gloves.

"And what might that be?" Elsa inquired.

"It's silly."

She raised an eyebrow at him.

Robert looked at her like he really didn't want to answer, but she knew she looked like an expectant professor awaiting an answer and he cowed under her glare.

"It's supposed to be...haunted." He whispered the last word not wanting to be overheard.

Elisa smiled. "I see." She glanced at Nef, who was back to leaning against the desk. He looked unamused.

Determined to be as professional as she could be with a ghost in the middle of the room, she changed the topic.

"I've just started on the four jars. They all need to be x-rayed and photographed, but we need a sample of the wrappings first for that chem analysis." Elisa pointed to the mummified body.

Robert glanced at the mummy and Elisa saw goosebumps pepper the flesh at the back of his neck.

"I don't think he'll mind," she smiled sarcastically. "But do take care to take as small a sample as you can and from an area that isn't too obvious, if you please."

Robert nodded. "Yes, Dr. Kent."

"Good. Do you mind if we listen to music while we work? I usually choose Chopin or something classical."

Robert shrugged, "No. I usually do, too. I don't mind classical."

Nef was working his way across the room. Elisa wasn't sure what he was up to, but she was shooting him silent warnings not to do anything to scare off the already skittish intern. She couldn't exactly ask him to back off, so she gave him her best stern professor look and went back to work.

Nef behaved. For a while.

Robert had just clipped a second piece of wrapping when the lights went off. His scream made Elisa's ears ring and she could hear Nef laughing. She rolled her eyes. It was going to be a long day.

Chapter Five

Elisa finally settled Robert enough to keep working, chalking up the lights to the automatic timer on them being broken. She wanted to tell Nef that sneaking into the tomb was a terrible idea, but Robert never left the room, and she didn't have an excuse to at the moment either. She had hoped Robert might go upstairs for lunch, but he ate a protein bar and kept working. At least his work ethic was intact. *He probably just wants to get this over with as soon as possible so he doesn't have to deal with the haunted lab.*

Just as that thought left her head, she saw Nef walk over to the microscope that was next to Robert and lift the arm very slowly. Robert caught the movement out of the corner of his eye and Elisa watched all of the color drain from his already pale face. She pretended to be working so that if he looked at her she could say she hadn't seen anything. He squeaked.

She didn't look up from her work but inclined her head in his direction. "Everything all right?"

Elisa heard a faintly mumbled *mmhmm* and decided now was a good time to excuse herself to her office for a little while. She hadn't finished what she was doing, and she was annoyed that she'd have to leave it halfway done, but she had to stop Nef from terrorizing Robert if she could. She was almost sure he was just trying to get her attention anyway.

She rose slowly and looked pointedly at Nef. Robert wasn't looking at her.

"I just need to go get something from my...uh, office. Back in a jiff."

When she was sure she was close enough to the door that Robert couldn't see her, she gestured wildly at Nef to go upstairs with her. He leaned against the table next to Robert and shook his head slightly.

Her ears got hot. *Damn him.* It's not like she could threaten or force him. She rolled her eyes and left the room anyway, silently hoping the entire elevator ride upstairs that Nef would do the decent thing and follow her.

She got lost three times trying to find her way to her office, but Nef was sitting behind her desk with his legs propped on it when she walked in.

"Bloody hell," she tried to keep her voice low since she'd already almost been caught talking to him earlier and closed the door for good measure. "You are as petulant as a child. Are you trying to give that poor boy a heart attack?"

His glower was replaced with a broad smile for once. It seemed to light his whole face up. She shuddered a little. She would not start thinking about how handsome he was. It was easier to relegate him to an anomaly when he wasn't right in front of her.

He raised an eyebrow at her.

"I'm flattered."

"I didn't say any..." she stepped further forward into the room as she trailed off.

"You didn't have to."

She'd been told that every emotion she felt showed on her face, that must have been what he'd meant.

"They do, but that's not it."

Her eyes widened in shock. "You can read my mind?"

"One of my many gifts." He smiled again, palms open in apology or self-aggrandizement, she wasn't sure.

He stood up and walked around the desk to stand in front of her. Elisa could have sworn she felt the air around her buzz when he got close to her.

"This whole time? You've been able to read my thoughts?"

A corner of his mouth twitched. "Yes. From the first moment, you saw me and thought I was...beautiful." He watched her face. "Another gift I'm thankful for. Women thought the same in my own time as well and told me often. And I'm flattered, as I said, but you know you're not really my type."

She made a face, "Because I'm curvy and short?"

Nef laughed, "No. Because you're alive."

That made her feel slightly better at least. She wondered briefly if she might have been his type if he'd been alive. Then regretted it the instant she was conscious of the thought.

He leaned a little closer to her, "I would think you would be any man's type in any era. Smart and beautiful are a rare combination."

Elisa blushed. "Thank you. But stay out of my head."

"You did say it wouldn't do to have you talking to someone who wasn't there. This can solve your problem."

"I like to keep my brain to myself as much as possible, thank you."

Nef raised an eyebrow at her and crossed his arms again. "I'll do my best, but your thoughts are so loud and often complicated. Especially when you're shouting at me downstairs."

She turned away from him to sit at her desk. "I'm glad you heard that because now I don't have to yell at you about Robert or the fact that trying to *sneak* into the Valley of Kings is a terrible, terrible idea."

"Yes, I know your position on both." He sighed. "I was just trying to have a little fun with him."

"Well don't," she hissed at him, still trying to keep her voice low.

There was a light tapping on her office door. She looked at Nef and rolled her eyes. *What now?*

"Come in," she said brightly.

"Elisa," Atef stepped in halfway and leaned on the door. "I was just going down to find you, but I'm glad you're here." He glanced around her office. Elisa looked with him. Nef had moved to stand behind her chair, but Atef hadn't noticed.

"What can I do for you, Atef?"

He put his hands in his pockets and looked back at her. "I know you've just started, and I hate to pull you away, but I was wondering if you might be free to visit a few of the dig sites from Friday to Monday. They have need of your expert services for a few mummies they've found and to read a few of the inscriptions on the tombs. Some of them are hieratic and they're having a hard time making them out. I hate to take your weekend, though."

Elisa wondered which dig site she might be going to. Saqqara was at least eight hours away. She smiled brightly at him. She was at his disposal and could hardly say no. This was what he was paying her for. Plus, it wasn't like she had a hot date or any plans.

"I'd be happy to. Where am I off to?" *Please say Thebes.*

"Just a quick jaunt over to the Valley. Four sites need you. I thought you could probably handle that in just a few days. I've booked you a flight on Friday morning if that works for you?"

Thank goodness.

Stop looking so relieved, came a male voice inside her head.

It took all of her willpower not to gasp and look back at Nef, but she nodded at Atef. "I don't think that will be a problem. Now that I have Robert helping downstairs, I can stand to be away for a few days without getting too behind."

Atef visibly relaxed. "So that's working out? He's doing well?"

"Worked right through lunch. He's a good kid."

"He is. I'm glad." Atef turned slowly and started walking toward the door. "Just out of curiosity, do you have any estimate of how long it might take you to finish up everything with our John Doe?"

She shook her head, unsure of the right answer. "Two months, maybe? There's not a whole lot to go through."

Atef seemed pleased by this and headed toward the hall.

Stall, came the voice again.

"Though the actual mummy might take more time."

He looked at her, maybe a little disappointed. "Take all the time you need, but I'd love weekly updates on your progress, hmm?"

"Of course," she said to his back as he walked out. He nodded to her before he closed the door.

Elisa waited a few minutes until he was out of what she considered ear shot.

"What was that about?"

Nef rubbed his goatee thoughtfully. "I'm not sure. Nothing good, though."

Elisa was a little stunned. "Wait. You can't read his mind?"

Nef paused and glanced at her, then turned back to the door. "No. Only yours. Just as only you can hear and see me."

"Huh. I guess you really are cursed."

Nef turned his attention back to her. "Another problem solved. You don't have to sneak into Thutmos' tomb now. You'll be welcomed with open arms."

He practically oozed with glee and charm now that he'd gotten what he wanted.

"A small blessing." Elisa rubbed her hands on her pant legs. She was going to have to be more careful not only of her thoughts but also with her conversations with Nef. She had the feeling Atef was starting to think she was a little crazy.

We could just communicate like this, Nef said in her mind.

Elisa shivered again and spoke softly to him. "No. Not unless you're invited. It's too...weird to hear you in my head." She stood up resolved to finish her tasks for the day. It was Tuesday, and there was a lot to get done before she was away for the weekend.

"I'm going back to the lab for a while. You can come, but only if you promise not to bother Robert anymore. Otherwise, I'll toss your mummy and the rest of you in the Nile and feed you to the crocodiles."

Nef had the good sense to look at least a little admonished and held his hands up in a gesture of surrender. Elisa nodded, pleased that she'd won that battle. At least for now.

The rest of the day passed quietly, with no more disturbances from Nef. He hung around the lab for a while and then disappeared for a few hours. She wondered briefly where he was when she first noticed he was gone. *Just wandering. I'll be back later. You're boring when you're thinking about measurements,* came his quiet reply.

Stay out of my head, she thought loudly.

He wasn't back by the time Robert left at five or when she was finally ready to pack up a few hours later. She contented herself with tidying the space and making her mental to-do list for tomorrow's artifacts. They had finished the canopic jars, nothing remarkable there, and the few shabti figures. There were fewer than she would have imagined, though. Since he'd been cursed, she supposed he was lucky he'd been left with any at all. None of them bore his name, just a common spell for a peaceful transition. She was ready to move on to the two larger clay jugs. Maybe there would be some shred of proof somewhere that would convince everyone else that Nef was the mummy that belonged to these items.

"What are you thinking?" Nef was beside her, but she hadn't noticed him, lost in thought as she was. She was startled enough that she almost dropped the tweezers and very expensive camera she was holding.

"Don't do that."

"You told me not to read your thoughts anymore, but it's not like I can make subtle noises to get your attention."

Elisa walked over to the cabinet and flung open the doors harder than she meant to. This wasn't working. She couldn't be startled by him every time she turned around, and she definitely didn't want him poking around in her thoughts all the time. She reached into the cabinet to put her things back where they belonged then turned to Nef.

"You can tell me, mentally, I guess, when you're here so I'm not dropping priceless artifacts when you happen to show up, but no poking around."

He leaned against the cabinet next to her. "That sounds like a fine compromise."

She had half-expected him to argue. The fact that he hadn't both relieved and deflated her a little.

"Good."

"Heading home?"

Elisa looked around in an "what does it look like I'm doing" way and he nodded.

"I'll see you tomorrow then."

He dematerialized in front of her eyes. *Maybe it's not too late to get that CAT scan*, she thought.

When she had cleaned up to her satisfaction, she hailed a cab and headed to the local market. Her phone had chimed and reminded her an hour ago that she needed to pick up cat food. She idly wondered if the cat was still there or if it had left to go back to wherever it had come from. The streets in Egypt were full of strays, but Bastet wasn't skittish or shy like others she'd seen lurking around her apartment. It seemed like the kind of cat that had been loved and taken care of before. Or was at least comfortable with humans.

Elisa stared at the choices of cat food in the market aisle. Why were there so many? She grabbed a few of each flavor and headed home. She had never been responsible for an animal before and didn't really know what Bastet might need. Should she have gotten a litter box? She had her key in the door and was about to turn around when she heard it meowing behind the door.

"I'm coming, I'm coming." Bastet greeted Elisa as soon she walked in. It twined itself around her legs several times while she tried to walk in. She realized while she was getting a plate out for its food that she really didn't know if Bastet was a girl or boy. She didn't think it mattered much, except that she didn't want baby Bastet's running around the apartment anytime soon.

Bastet was obviously hungry and jumped up on the counter before Elisa had a chance to put the plate on the floor. It made happy noises as it devoured the cat food on the plate. Elisa petted it while she picked up her phone and Googled "how to tell the sex of a cat." The top answer was to look at the cat's bottom. Round for male, vertical slit for female. Elisa eyed the cat's bottom carefully. Its tail was down, so she'd have to lift it in order to do her inspection.

Bastet was still eating while Elisa rubbed down its back. "Come on, Kent. You inspect dead bodies for a living. This isn't any different." *Except dead bodies didn't have claws*, she reminded herself. She lifted the tail gently and took a peek. Vertical slit. Bastet was completely unbothered, and Elisa sighed in relief.

"Well, at least I don't have to change your name. Not that you'd know you were named after a goddess even if you were a boy." Bastet finished her dinner, licked her lips, and then pushed her head against Elisa's chin. She purred noisily. Elisa picked her up and snuggled her then carried her into her bedroom. She'd take a shower, eat something, then go to bed. Having to guard her thoughts from Nef and think only of work had been more exhausting than she anticipated.

Bastet waited for her on the bed while she showered and while she ate. When she pulled the comforter over her, the cat settled happily on her stomach and fell asleep. Elisa lay awake for a while longer thinking about Thutmoses' tomb and, if there was time, how she was going to manage to get in there without arousing suspicion. Her mind wandered to Nef and about what it must have been like for him the last hundred and thirty years to be so separated from the life he knew and only interacting with a handful of people. They had that last bit in common.

When she finally drifted off to sleep, she pictured Nef's rare smile and not her parents for once.

Chapter Six

The next day passed much in the same way Tuesday had. Nef hung around until he got bored and then wandered around the museum while Robert and Elisa worked. He'd started announcing his presence in her mind so that she wasn't as surprised when he appeared out of nowhere. She took a lunch break in the middle of the day to retreat to her office for a bit. Nef inevitably found her. He eventually turned the conversation to Thutmose's tomb and why he needed to go with her.

"We've been over this. I haven't even decided if I'm going to help you or not. I don't know how to get you in. Can't you just tell me what I'm looking for?" Elisa argued.

"It's been almost four-thousand years since I've been there. I can't just draw you a map. And what if he changed where it was? He was pharaoh for another few decades after I died, remember?"

His logic was reasonable, but Elisa was no closer to coming up with a solution to their problem. She'd thought about ordering some kind of personal camera and live feeding to the lab computer, but there was no way to do that without the risk of Robert seeing, and online ordering wasn't good enough here to get something like that to her the next day.

Elisa paced her office as she thought. She knew that his spirit was tied to his remains—wherever he went they went. She briefly thought about just taking a piece of him with her but dismissed it just as quickly.

"No, wait. Go back to that thought," he'd been watching her pace from the leather sofa.

She glared at him. "You said you were going to stay out of my head."

"I have," he growled. "But you're so loud. You like to listen to music while you work, right?"

"What does that have to do with anything?"

"You can tune it out when you want to, when you're focused on something else, right? But if someone turns up the volume it's harder to ignore and can become a...nuisance while you're working, yes?"

Elisa caught on to the metaphor. "I'm sorry I'm such a nuisance," she said, dejected, and walked around to her desk.

He looked admonishingly at her. "That is not what I meant. You're just hard to ignore sometimes." Elisa barely caught the dark look he sent her sent a wave of desire straight to her belly and she cleared her throat to get herself together.

"I'm not taking a *piece* of you to the dig with me. We don't even know if that would work. You're very fortunate not to be in pieces anyway. Most mummies that I see have lost fingers, toes, arms, genitalia," she said pointedly.

He had the good sense to look appalled and crossed his legs. She chuckled. Apparently, some things never changed.

"Despite that," he said as he rubbed his chin, "no one would notice. It's also my body and I'm giving you permission. Besides, how do you know I'm not in pieces? You haven't examined my corpse yet. I could have fallen to shreds by now."

She shook her head and laughed. She appreciated that he was trying to lighten the mood, even at his own expense. "I looked over your x-rays and your body the first day I was here. Not thoroughly, but I surely would have noticed if some part of you had fallen off."

"Why don't we go check?"

Elisa didn't have an answer for that, so she made her way downstairs. She was surprised when he got on the elevator with her rather than just popping from place to place like he normally did.

"Robert is still down there. He knows we're not examining the body for a few more weeks. What am I going to tell him?"

Nef stood at her shoulder. She realized they'd never stood this close to each other before. He was at least a foot taller than she was. Not that that was hard. At only 5'3 most people were taller than she was.

"Send him off on an errand. He's an intern, yes? Have him get you a coffee or find a file."

Elisa scowled. She'd had a boss like that on a dig site one time and hated him. She'd been his errand girl and she'd vowed to never do that to anyone. Still, she could come up with something.

They walked into the lab and Robert was just putting the jug he'd been working on back on the shelf that had become its home for the time being.

Good timing, Nef said in her ear.

Elisa walked in, trying to project more confidence than she felt. She looked at Nef's body to the left of the room, covered in linen, then back to Robert.

"Robert?" He glanced up at her as he was grabbing the next jar to be cataloged. "I was wondering if you might do me a favor."

"Sure, Dr. Kent. Anything you need." His smile was warm and genuine.

His warmth made her feel even more guilty for what she was about to do. "Since you're more familiar with the labs than I am, I was wondering if you might go to the Hatshepsut artifacts for me and get item 221B. I'd like to compare it to the jars here and see if we have a similar style and then create a timeline."

Robert removed his gloves and his lab coat and set them aside. "221...B? Sure thing. I'll be right back."

"Thanks so much." Elisa smiled at him as he passed and moved out of the way of the door.

After he left, Nef followed her to where his body lay. "What's a...221B?"

Elisa bent over to examine Nef's mummified corpse as closely as she dared. She started at his head. "There is no 221B. It's the address of one of my favorite book characters."

Nef laughed outright. The sound was pleasant and almost seductive. Elisa looked up at him and smiled, then got back to the task at hand. "I don't know how long it will take him to realize it, but I figure I've got at least a few minutes."

After taking a cursory glance under the aged wrappings and then at the completely intact body of Nef, which was a little disconcerting with his ghost standing right beside her, Elisa donned a pair of latex gloves to gently move some things around. Not only was she looking for a piece that might be unattached, but also wouldn't be missed and was small enough to transport.

She looked closer. Elisa could tell even after this many years that he had been wrapped with care. The linen was frail in some places, but the wrappings were even and thick. He smelled of resin—frankincense and myrrh if she wasn't mistaken, and some other scent she couldn't identify—when she got close to him. It was an exotic combination and she was pleased that he had been so well preserved. She didn't want to unwrap any part of him but knew she would eventually have to anyway. Elisa had been hoping to put that off as long as possible.

"Does it bother you?" She asked while he looked closely at his right hand. There were still rings visible on his fingers under the wrappings.

He watched her but didn't look at her. "It used to. It doesn't anymore. It just is." He walked around his body over to her. "I was angry for a long time. I still am some days. Not just that I was murdered but that Thutmose would do something so dishonorable to someone he considered a 'brother.' To us, it's the ultimate betrayal."

Elisa looked up at him as he ran a transparent finger down his own mummified linen. "Whoever performed the rituals on you must have thought highly of you, though. They did a beautiful job."

Elisa stood up and looked at him. He kept looking down at himself, seemingly lost in his own thoughts. "I knew them. I was respected. They would have treated me with kindness and reverence. I imagine to everyone else it must have just seemed like I died mysteriously, not that Thutmose had me murdered." She felt his gaze on her before he cleared his throat and said, "It's cedar, by the way. Not bitumen."

"Cedar? Imported then."

"Yes, from Jubayl. Gubla. That's in Lebanon now, though we didn't call it that then. We were a rich and vast nation."

"Huh. I never would have guessed. Robert's work will confirm that." Elisa bent back to her work and rubbed a finger carelessly over Nef's mummified jaw. Maybe she could take a tooth. "Poison is a woman's method of death." She had said it idly, as one of the many random facts that percolated in her brain.

Nef was quiet. When she turned her head to look at him, the scowl was back.

"What's wrong?"

"What you said. I hadn't given any other possibility than Thutmos much thought. He likely would have faced me himself." Nef walked away from the table and over to the shelves. "Why would she?"

Elisa didn't have to ask who he meant. The woman, Neferaue, who had lied to him to try to save herself then disappeared.

She busied herself with continuing to look over his body while he stood silently and contemplated unwrapping the top of the head. If she did, she'd have to wrap it back quickly and there was no way of knowing how many layers were there or if she'd be able to put it back before Robert came in.

"Oh, for Ra's sake," Nef said, exasperated, from behind her. He walked over to his own body and jerked the thumb right off. He tossed it unceremoniously at a horrified Elisa.

"I can't believe you just did that! How did you just do that?"

Nef sat down, a little less visible than usual.

"With great effort. But you have your piece. No one will notice. You're the only one who looks at me anyway. You're going to take all of my bindings off soon. I'm sure you can cover it up later."

Elisa seethed. She was speechless as she looked from the mummy back to its owner. She bent down to examine the damage he'd done, but nothing was immediately visible. His thumbs had been tucked under the rest of his digits to begin with. No one who glanced at the mummy would notice anything different.

She huffed over to the closet where the preservation equipment was kept and retrieved a small white box with a cotton liner. She turned around to give him a piece of her mind, but when she looked at him, he was pale with a sheen of sweat on his forehead. He was rubbing the crease between his eyebrows with the still intact ghost-thumb. Did ghosts sweat?

"Why are you so pale?" She set the box on the table and bent down in front of him.

Nef kept his eyes closed. "Moving objects takes a lot of effort and concentration. It tires me." He finally did open his eyes and looked at her. Their faces were close. She could see the despair and anguish in his eyes. They were chestnut brown and lovely with flecks of light brown, almost gold, around the iris.

It had been easy to be dismissive of him. He wasn't *real*. Whether she found his heart had mattered to her only from an archeological perspective, but now she realized that even though his body wasn't here, he was as real as she was. He still had emotions and feelings that she hadn't given a second thought to. He'd come to her knowing she could, and probably would, say no to him. Guilt and pity washed over her.

"Nef, I–"

"Don't." He moved to put his hand over hers on the table and she almost felt him. The air around her hand felt warmer and buzzed as if electrified. He seemed just as startled by the contact and movement as she was. His eyes widened and he moved his hand away and back to his forehead. "It's been a long afternoon. I just need to rest."

She started to say something else, to apologize, but he was gone before she could, and she was left staring at an empty chair.

Chapter Seven

Elisa still hadn't seen or heard from Nef by Thursday afternoon. She hadn't wanted him to join her at the dig, but she didn't want to leave things like this either. She chided herself for her aloofness. If she hadn't said anything about being poisoned or made a decision about which piece of him to take sooner, they might still be talking. It wasn't that she couldn't empathize, but the rational part of her always took over before her emotional side. Then again, she wasn't sure anyone could be fully expected to empathize with someone who had been dead for 3,500 years and had been killed and betrayed by either their brother or their lover.

She knew what it was to be left behind though. If she couldn't find any other common ground between them, they at least had that. She thought about how painful it had been to live life in the shadow of her family legacy but also to have lived when they didn't. To experience life in a way they couldn't any longer. To be the last one carrying her name. She tried to put herself in Nef's situation, but just couldn't imagine being the last one left to see what had happened to the world after so many centuries. He had been carrying his anger and betrayal around with him for as long with no way to fix it himself.

For once in her life, it seemed she was the one holding all the power. She could turn him down and doom him to a life that was spent watching the world pass by from museum windows. Or, she could try to help set him free. It wouldn't cost her anything. It might cost her her pride if she got fired. Or her reputation if Atef or Robert thought she was crazy, but those seemed minor in comparison to Nef's stakes. She didn't want another job, but she could get one. There had been about twenty offers, it was just that the GEM was her dream. Jobs, though, were a dime a dozen. Nef only had one life, er, afterlife.

As had become her new habit over the last few days, she went up to her office for her lunch hour. She had worked herself into a mood and sat down at her desk with her head in her hands. Crying seemed a little over the top, but she couldn't stop the tear that rolled down her cheek.

Nef's voice sounded softly from across the room. "I hope those tears aren't for me."

Elisa looked up. He was sitting on the leather sofa with his elbows resting on his knees. His fingers were steepled in front of his mouth. He looked more visible today than he had yesterday; almost back to his full color. His hair was pulled back again and he had on jeans, loafers, and a blue t-shirt. He looked like he was posing for an Armani ad.

Elisa swiped at the tear and sat up a little straighter. "I... wanted to tell you I'm sorry. I was rude and inconsiderate. I'm not used to having someone's literal life in my hands. I'm not good with people. I know that. I drive people away because I'm awkward and I always say the wrong thing." Once she'd got going, her words came out in a torrent. She finally paused to take a breath and realized she should have just stopped with the apology. "I'm sorry."

"Elisa Kent, you didn't drive me away. I needed to rest and I needed time to think about what you said. It may have been a little thoughtless, but then, I think I have been, too. I shouldn't have expected that you would be as willing to accept me as your great-grandfather was. Perhaps I should have eased you in a little more to my situation, but I've found that it's easier to rip the band-aid off, so to speak."

Nef stood up and walked over to her. He sat on the edge of her desk and looked down at her. "I will accept your apology if you will accept mine. In my previous life, what I said and did was obeyed without question. It's taking some getting used to in this life that that isn't the case any longer."

He lifted a hand as if to wipe away another tear that had escaped her bottom lid, then stopped before he got to her face. "I didn't mean to make you cry. Tears are quite becoming on you, though."

Elisa rolled her eyes. "I'm not sure tears are becoming on anyone. They make my face blotchy and red puffy, and my freckles stand out."

"I quite like your...freckles." The word sounded funny when he said it as if he never had before. "Can we be friends again?"

Elisa nodded and a corner of her mouth turned up. "I'm actually glad you were up here. I accept your logic about you somehow coming along. We need to figure out a way to test this hypothesis of you being attached to a body part. We're leaving tomorrow morning and we don't even know if it'll work. I'm going to be pissed if you ripped your thumb off for no good reason."

Nef smiled and looked at his hands. "There's that indignity I've grown so fond of."

What's with all the flattery today? She wondered.

He didn't acknowledge that he'd heard that particular thought, but when he looked at her again, something had changed in his eyes.

"I have an idea about that. I don't know if my spirit is tied to my body or the heart scarab. The scarab contains the spell that makes me visible to the reader. It creates a connection of sorts, but I exist in this form whether it's read or not. As far as I know, the scarab hasn't been separated from my body since I was discovered in 1886."

"So you want me to take both?" Elisa paled this time.

"I know. I know you'd rather not. But can we at least try?"

"Try smuggling not one, but maybe *two* priceless artifacts from the largest and most secure collection in the known world? Sure. No big deal."

Nef clapped his hands on his thighs and stood up. Elisa was sure her sarcasm hadn't been lost on him, but he was moving toward the door like he was taking her seriously.

"Now?"

"Why not?"

"Because Robert has been back in the lab and he's not too happy about the hunt I sent him on yesterday. I played it off, badly, but he's giving me the silent treatment today."

"Maybe it's not because of that. You looked sullen all morning. He was probably just giving you space."

"You were down there this morning?"

"I was. You were too deep in thought and self-loathing to notice, so I came up here. I figured you'd come up eventually."

Nef might have been dead, but he was no less infuriating for that, and, she hated to admit, kind of sweet. Elisa sighed.

"I will help you. I meant to say that with my apology. Not that you're really giving me much of a choice, because it seems you're likely to annoy me to death if I don't. I'll smuggle you out after hours tonight to test this insane theory and I'll do my best to find your heart and the scroll."

Nef's smile was so wide that it actually reached his eyes this time. Elisa was fascinated by it. No wonder everyone did what he'd said when he was alive.

"I knew you'd come to see things my way eventually."

Pfft, she thought loudly.

I heard that, came his quick reply.

Elisa got up and went to wait for Robert to leave so she could become a thief for the first time in her life.

What felt like an eternity later, Robert finally left for the day. Elisa had tried to act as normal as she could with the prospect of committing a crime in her immediate future. When it was time, she gathered the heart scarab and the white box containing Nef's thumb and wrapped them together in a little linen scrap, and placed them gently in her bag.

"Ready?" Nef asked.

"Not really, but I'm committed now." Elisa tried to shake the anxiety away by flexing her fingers, but it lingered. She'd left late a few times and had yet to run anyone. She hoped that luck would continue.

She paused at the door. "How will we know if it's working?"

"I'll be next to you the whole time. I think if I start to fade and you can't hear me we'll know we've been unsuccessful."

"Right." Elisa opened the door and Nef followed. She walked into the hall, down the corridor, and out to the staff parking lot and cab stand across from it. When she hailed a cab, Nef was still next to her. When she got in, he remained just as visible as he always had been.

Seems to be working. What now? she whispered in her mind.

Is this an invitation to talk to like this?

Yes, of course. I can't exactly talk to nothing in front of the driver.

I could talk. He wouldn't hear me. Nef smiled and started waving his hands in front of the rearview mirror and screaming.

Elisa tried to remain as neutral as possible and looked out the window.

See?

You're insane, she thought intensely. *I guess we'll go to my apartment. See how long this lasts.*

Are you always so forward on the first date?

You've seen too many movies.

As if I've had anything else to do.

She *tsked* at him loudly and the diver looked at her in the mirror and asked in Arabic if she was alright.

"Na'aam. Shukran." *Yes, thank you.* Elisa gave him the address to her apartment, and they were there within minutes.

She walked up the three flights of stairs and opened her door. Nef had followed behind her silent but grinning the whole way.

Bastet greeted Elisa when she walked in.

"You have a cat," Nef exclaimed. She turned to him because she wasn't sure if it was an afraid exclamation or an excited one. When she saw the expression on his face, she realized it was excitement.

"I love cats!"

"I thought dead Egyptians hated cats," she moved into the living room to put her bag down, but Bastet stayed where she was at the door next to Nef.

"What gave you that idea?"

"A movie."

"Ah. Now who has seen too many films? Not true at all. What's her name?"

"Bastet." The cat hadn't seemed surprised that she was talking to nothing, but at the mention of her name, she looked up at Nef and meowed.

"Can she see you?" Elisa wasn't sure what to think of this development.

"I'm not sure, but she's looking right at me. Hello, little mother."

Bastet meowed at him again and tried to greet him the same way she greeted Elisa by rubbing around his legs.

"Where did you get her?" Nef was curious about this too.

"She just showed up on Monday after I got home." Elisa chose not to regale him with the tale of how she'd scared herself more than the cat and instead went through the motions of feeding Bastet and then scrounging around in the fridge for something for herself. She settled on a container of cottage cheese.

Nef watched her from the doorway. "Do you ever eat a real meal? I've only ever seen you drink coffee and snack on those bars and cheese."

Elisa had been self-conscious about her weight since someone in college had called her "fluffy." She was a size 10, but she was still larger than most of her colleagues.

"I eat. I just haven't had time to shop much since I got here."

Nef looked around the apartment. The walls were bare, the furniture looked like it hadn't been touched. "Or do much else from the looks of things. Do you mind if I look around?"

She lifted a shoulder, "Make yourself at home." Elisa wasn't sure how she felt about someone looking around her space, but he'd poked around in her mind, and she remembered how much he seemed to enjoy looking around the museum. She put the lid back on her cottage cheese and followed him into her office. He was standing in the middle of the room and looked distinctly out of place amidst her boxes and books.

"Wow."

"What?"

"Do you collect books?" He seemed impressed.

"Not really. I just like to read. Books are comforting." *And they're always there, unchanging,* she thought to herself.

"Have you read all of these?" Nef walked over to her multi-volume Shakespeare to inspect the titles. "They're all…alphabetized in the boxes."

Elisa tried not to look sheepish. "Currently by author. Sometimes by title. That way I know where everything is. But, yes, I've read them. Most of them multiple times. Some of them not at all." Elisa picked up her favorite copy of *A Midsummer Night's Dream* and stroked the spine. She really needed to get some shelves up.

"You're going to have a beautiful library in here someday."

"I hope so. They go pretty much everywhere I go, so if I ever leave, the library will come down too."

"Are you already planning on leaving?" Nef walked over to her and looked genuinely curious as to what her answer might be.

"No, not yet, but I doubt I'll stay here forever."

"You don't want to put down roots somewhere?"

Elisa was starting to get uncomfortable with the direction of this conversation. She backed out of the room and turned toward her bedroom. "I need to pack," she called over her shoulder. "Feel free to keep wandering."

The diversion of packing gave her a few minutes to collect herself. Why did he make her so uncomfortable? Did it matter if she spilled her secrets to him? Did he know all of them already? She hadn't let anyone alive into her life in too long. Maybe sharing them with someone less than living would be nice. She couldn't exactly scare him off and he couldn't die...again, so maybe it would be okay.

Unless you send him back to the afterlife somehow.

The thought came to her unwelcome and unwanted. They had formed a weird sort of bond with each other in a few short days. Or at least some kind of understanding. She reminded herself that the chances of finding what they were looking for were remote and being able to actually complete some sort of spell was almost laughable, but she had told him she'd try.

With her bag unceremoniously packed for a dig weekend, she walked back into the living room to find Nef and Bastet watching each other intently.

"You're still here. I guess something we've done has worked."

Nef *hmmmed* at her. Bastet had jumped up on the side table that held a few photos and Nef's attention was drawn to the one of her with her parents.

"Is that you?"

Elisa leaned against the sofa. "Yeah. With my parents." She picked up the photo as she had done so many times before and touched their faces.

"Where are they?"

She looked up at him, confused. "Don't you already know?"

"No. Should I?" Realization seemed to dawn on him. "I can only read the thoughts you're currently thinking. Not every thought you've ever had. I don't know everything that has happened in your life."

She didn't know why, but she believed him. If he'd known, he wouldn't have asked.

He inclined his head toward the picture. "Will you tell me about them?"

"They were wonderful. They died when I was sixteen. They were Egyptologists, too." Elisa slid onto the sofa and Nef sat on the other side. She told him about what it was like to grow up going from dig site to dig site, always exploring. The excitement of a new discovery that someone hadn't seen in 4,000 years. She told him about how much they loved her. How they had died and she had gone to live with her eccentric aunt in England. She told him how she'd felt most at home among ancient things and while she'd tried to be interested in literature and other subjects, nothing ever quite called to her the way the history of Egypt did. She opened up to him about the pressure of the legacy of the four Egyptologists she descended from and the need to make her own name.

Nef sat and listened intently. He never interrupted, only watched her, and made noises that confirmed his attention. When she had finished quite sometime later, he circled back to a similar question he'd asked earlier.

"So no husband or even boyfriend? You didn't mention anyone."

What the hell? I've told him all this already.

"No. I dated a guy in college my second year. I was eighteen, he was twenty. I fell madly in love with him. His mom had died a few years before and we consoled each other over that. I thought I could really be myself around him, awkward as I am. He was also interested in Egyptology, but he got a job offer right after graduation and took it. He told me his career was more important than a relationship. Broke up with me on the spot. That's when I realized that everyone eventually leaves," she finished quietly.

Bastet chose that moment to jump into her lap and nuzzle Elisa on the chin. "I haven't really gotten close to any one since then."

"That must make for a lonely existence."

Elisa rubbed Bastet under the chin. "Funny. I was thinking the same thing about you earlier this morning."

Nef raised his eyebrows and shrugged. "It hasn't been everything I thought it would be. This has been a strange sort of afterlife. It does get lonely. I've been fortunate in the people I've been able to communicate with over the years, but there have only been four that didn't run screaming when I appeared to them. And only two that I've really gotten to know. I'm thankful for the time and friendship your great-grandfather gave me while he could." He looked at her with a gleam in his eye. "I'm also thankful for you. For believing me, even if you're logic tells you you shouldn't."

Not one to take compliments, Elisa changed the subject. "Will you tell me about him?" Elisa asked sleepily.

Nef told her about Charles Kent, how he'd been funny and irreverent, a little eccentric—seemed like it ran in the family—and clearly ahead of his time. He filled in the gaps on how he watched the chaos of WWII from the windows of a museum in Luxor. He went back further and told her about his childhood, his favorite foods, how he missed touching, tasting, smelling. He told her what Thutmos had been like as a child. She laughed when he told her a few tales of times they'd gotten in trouble and teared up when he told her of the war, famine, cruelty, and death he'd seen. She started to drift off when he was telling her about the Assyrians, but if he noticed, he didn't say anything. Lulled into the comfort of his voice and having shed a weight she'd borne too long, she fell asleep on her sofa with the cat softly purring in her lap.

Elisa woke up and light was streaming through the balcony doors. A blanket had been pulled over her while she slept. She would have to remember to thank Nef for that. She couldn't imagine the amount of effort that must have taken him. She glanced at the other end of the sofa where he'd been and saw that he was still there. His eyes were closed and he snored softly. He looked so peaceful when he slept. The scowl that had been ever-present in their first few days together had disappeared like it had never been. His eyelashes and hair gleamed a blue-black in the sunlight. She'd half expected him to disappear in the middle of the night. To where, she had no idea.

Bastet meowed at her and broke her focus on him. Clearly, the cat didn't care that there was a gorgeous, sleeping man on the sofa. She wanted breakfast. Elisa checked the time on her phone and stretched. She still had a few hours before she had to be at the airport. Enough time to get coffee and maybe eat a real breakfast. Thankfully the flight was only about an hour so she'd be to the Valley before lunch. She wanted to get her consults over with so she and Nef had time to explore the tomb before she had to come back. Hopefully, the travel wouldn't wear Nef out, but so far, all seemed fine.

Elisa got up quietly and moved into the kitchen to feed the demanding cat. She tried to make as little noise as possible. She didn't know if Nef was a hard sleeper or not. Hell, she hadn't known ghosts slept at all.

She wanted a warm shower before she spent several days in a dig house in the desert and only got cold ones, so she made her way to her tiny bathroom and lingered under the spray thinking about her conversation with Nef. Talking to him had been easy. He didn't have any expectations. He just wanted to get to know her. Out of curiosity or simply because of circumstance, she wasn't sure. The handful of dates she'd been on in the last few years had only ever been about sex or networking. It was nice not to have any pretenses.

She had just turned off the shower and was reaching for her towel when she heard Nef call out to her.

"Elisa, I–"

He stopped as soon as he saw her. Elisa was too shocked to remember to grab her towel so she just stood, naked and dripping while he gawked at her. His eyes traveled slowly over her body. As his gaze took her in, she could feel herself warming from her head to her toes. Her senses came back to her when he finally met her eyes. There was a hunger there that was so powerful it almost scared her. She quickly reached for her towel and threw it over her front. It was too late to preserve any shred of modesty, but she still took her time wrapping it around herself and securing it in place.

Nef was watching her. He hadn't spoken or moved. Elisa crossed to the mirror, then turned on him.

"What? Why are you looking at me like that?"

Nef walked to her slowly and stood behind her. She turned around to face him ready to be defensive. He was so close that if he had been alive, they would have been touching. She looked into eyes so dark they were almost black. The air around her was warm and carried with it a hint of frankincense. She stared at his lips and the pulse in her neck throbbed.

When he finally spoke, his voice was hoarse. "Because you're beautiful. If only you knew what I wanted to do with you right now."

Despite the heat of her shower and the room, a chill ran over her. She swallowed hard.

"That's only because you've been celibate for three-thousand years."

"Don't," he stopped her. "Don't do that. That's not the reason."

No man had ever looked at her the way Nef was looking at her now. She indulged herself and imagined his full lips trailing kisses down her wet body and closed her eyes, lost in that moment.

Her phone rang. She picked it up and answered too loudly. Her attention wasn't on what she was hearing, but she still affirmed and then hung up.

"That was the car service," she whispered, still looking at his lips. "They'll be here in twenty minutes."

Nef was still looking at her. He hadn't moved and she didn't know what would happen if she tried to walk through him.

"Elisa," he breathed. She looked into his eyes again. "Just be still for a minute."

She didn't know what she expected him to do, but it certainly wasn't what he did. He bent his head and touched his lips to hers. Elisa felt the slightest tingle where his lips were and desire snaked its way into her belly. She didn't think about anything but him, about what his hands would feel like on her hips, wrapped in her hair.

The tingle stopped and she opened her eyes to find that he had pulled away.

"I'll let you get dressed." He turned and walked out of the bathroom but not before turning and looking at her. Elisa could have sworn that she saw sadness in his eyes.

Chapter Eight

The plane ride had been uneventful, except that Elisa couldn't stop touching her lips and thinking about the way they had tingled when he'd kissed her. *But it wasn't a real kiss because he's not real,* she chastised herself. Nef had been silent in the car and had disappeared as soon as she got on the plane. She briefly wondered why but was also grateful for the space it gave her to think and breathe.

Are you still here?

Always, came his quick reply in her head.

She tried to stop thinking about what their almost-kiss had felt like because she knew he could read her thoughts, so she picked up the most boring book she'd brought with her and tried to read that instead.

The ride to the site was hot and dusty even with all of the windows rolled down in the ancient SUV. If she hadn't known better, she'd thought they were driving to the middle of nowhere, but suddenly the mountains and valleys she knew so well started appearing as if a mirage in the middle of the flat desert. The curves of ancient sand and rock stood as a beacon now for those who came to learn and those who came to honor the history of what had once been the glory of Egypt. It never failed to impress her.

I remember leaving here so long ago, Nef finally broke his silence in her mind. She cautiously glanced back at him in the backseat and saw that same sense of wonder she thought was reflected in her own face.

Did you come here often when you were alive?

As much as was needed. It looked quite different then. This is a shell of what once was.

They pulled into the designated space and Paoula, the director of the current dig walked up and embraced Elisa.

"I'm so happy to see you! It's been too long."

Elisa, a little startled, gently patted Paoula's shoulder. "It's good to see you, too," she gently pulled back, "It's only been a few years."

Paoula had her beautiful jet-black hair pulled into a ponytail at the nape of her neck and was wearing her customary "desert fatigues" as she called them. Now the director of this dig site and a professor for Jaen University, Paoula had known Elisa's parents and had frequently done digs with them in various locations all over Egypt. Despite a life mostly lived under tents, she didn't look like she'd aged a day since Elisa was a girl.

"I'm not used to seeing you so infrequently. Let me look at you," Paoula put her hands on Elisa's shoulders and held her back a little, examining her as if she were an ancient mummy herself.

"Nothing different. Nothing interesting," Elisa assured her.

"Nonsense. You look happy."

Elisa's smile was honest. "I am. How could I not be?"

"You have earned yourself a very distinguished position. Your parents would be proud."

"Your letter of recommendation certainly helped."

"It was the least I could do," Paoula smiled a little sadly, thoughts seeming to flit across her features that Elisa couldn't place. Paoula opened her hands wide and raised her eyebrows, "Well. Let me show you around, madam curator. We have several interesting things that need your expertise."

Elisa looked behind her and saw Nef, looking a little like a lost puppy. *Do you want to look around?* She asked in her head.

Perhaps. If I do, I'll stay close. I'm not sure how far I can go anyway.

Before she knew it, he had dematerialized going in the opposite direction she and Paoula were going. A temporary pavilion had been set up outside of one of the tombs and stacks of crates filled with plastic bags labeled meticulously were gathered there. Tables of archeological students were gathered around measuring and cataloging.

"I have some things for you to see out here later, but the body is still inside the tomb, so I'll show you that first. I have to warn you, it's a bit of a tight fit in there, so you may want to leave your bag here." Paoula gestured to Elisa's pack and she set it under one of the tables in the tent. She grabbed a few of her tools and a headlamp before she left it.

A hole had been dug into the side of the mountain for a makeshift door and metal bars and mesh had been set up so that the metal door attached to it could be locked. Grave robbers were still an issue, even today, especially at newly discovered sites. Elisa noted that this was tomb number 68 before she walked in and jotted it in her notebook.

The corridor was just like many others she'd entered. Carved steps led down an opening about six feet wide before the steps began to narrow. The ancient Egyptians had carved miles and miles of tunnels into the earth to attempt to hide their pharaohs and their riches. Each tomb usually contained an ante chamber and then a slightly larger room attached to it. Some pharaohs were buried with their families or priests near them to aid them in the transition to the afterlife. There could be miles separating the tombs from one another in these tunnels, and some had been well hidden. Modern technology like LIDAR had helped uncover tombs that had been previously undiscovered.

After walking for about thirty minutes, Paoula finally stopped. There was a hole in the floor that Elisa might have fallen into if she hadn't been paying attention. A small wooden ladder was poking out of it. She looked down.

"Well that's unusual."

Paoula looked triumphant. "I know. First one that's been found like this. We can only fit one at a time, so I'll let you have a look. I'll be up here if you need anything, but take your time."

Elisa had the same jitters she always had at a dig like this when she climbed down the ladder. The anticipation of discovery she supposed. Small, portable work lights had been set up below, but she turned her headlamp on just the same. The stone beneath her was almost cold as her knuckles brushed against it and the air around her was cool enough. Excellent conditions for preservation, despite the temperatures outside in the summer.

At the base of the ladder, she turned around to find a small chamber. It was tall enough to stand up in and the contents had been emptied. She knew that anything that was in this room was outside under the shelter. At the end of the small room, a small rectangular hole had been dug out. She looked at her hips and back at the opening, mentally calculating if she could squeeze through. Getting stuck in an ancient tomb was not her idea of a good day. She walked about five steps and crouched down. The tunnel was longer than she'd imagined. She'd have to slither through on her belly. She hoped it was dug out a little better on the other side.

"Right. No time like the present," she said to herself as she got on her hands and knees and army-crawled her way through. Her hips and lower back brushed the tops and sides but she was able to clear the space. It took her a few minutes to wiggle to the end where she could see a wooden box in front of her.

The area where the sarcophagus sat was large enough to crouch in, but just barely. Maintaining structural integrity was paramount in tombs like this so that nothing collapsed and ruined the artifacts within. The workers must have dug out as much as they thought they safely could, but it was no wonder the heavy wooden sarcophagus stayed where it was.

Elisa could barely make out the writing on the outside of the tomb. Nothing looked too familiar. *Damn.* She took a small brush out and brushed some of the dirt and dust off of the side. It appeared to be Meroitic, a newer writing system used by the Egyptians in the 2nd century. This tomb had been placed here more recently than the others, then. Her specialty was Hieratic and Hieroglyphics with a little bit of Demotic and Coptic thrown in for good measure. There were very few who could read Meroitic with any sense of certainty, and she wasn't going to try, especially not in these conditions.

She peered into the coffin and saw the largely eroded wrappings of a mummy. The style of mummification confirmed her suspicions about the period. The Greeks practiced a different type of mummification that was often less precise than that of the ancient Egyptians, and when Alexander conquered the world, this style became the norm.

Only the wrappings on the upper body and one femur remained, so she was able to get a good look at the bones underneath. She very carefully moved the fabric away from the hips so she could get an idea of the gender of this skeleton. Mature male and female skeletons had very precise differences, but because the mortality age in earlier centuries had been so young, it was often hard to tell the difference between adolescent males and females.

Elisa carefully examined the femur, pelvis, and a few vertebrae that she could see. An image started forming in her mind of who this person was, as it often did when her fingertips connected with the bones of the deceased. This was a curious specimen indeed. She took out her pocket notebook and measuring tape and made some notes for herself. Once she was satisfied that her suspicions were confirmed on paper, she made her way back out. She had been in the tomb less than thirty minutes.

The air in the antechamber was clearer and she breathed in a few good lungfuls before heading back up to Paoula who sat waiting for her in the outermost chambered hallway.

She looked up from her book and smiled at Elisa, "That didn't take long."

Elisa shrugged but a smile crept in, "Expert, remember?"

Paoula stood and stretched. "I remember. So? Anything interesting?"

"Mmmm," Elisa glanced back down into the pit. "What pharaoh did they find here?"

"One of Seti's sons and some of his family. Why?"

"Interesting." Seti had been buried about a thousand years before this coffin would have been here. Not related then. "It's a woman. I'd guess about seventy-two years old based on the ossification and osteoporosis of her spine. The writing on the sarcophagus is Meroitic, which I am definitely not an expert in. The mummification is in the Greek style, which confirms that same timeline. But who she was and why she's here, I have no idea. Are you going to be able to move her out?"

Paoula raised an eyebrow at all the information Elisa had just relayed. "Do you know that our best archeologist was in there for three hours and didn't come out with half of what you just told me? He assumed the writing was hieratic."

"A common misconception. The cursive is similar, but there are distinct differences."

"Your brain astounds me," Paoula wrapped an arm around Elisa's shoulders and began the trek back up with her. "As to moving her...we'll have to see. We're not convinced the inner chamber will sustain much more digging, but I'm hopeful we'll be able to get her out and solve this new mystery you've just handed us."

Elisa glanced back down at the tomb. "It's such a privilege, what we do. To be able to be the first human eyes on something undiscovered for so long. To try to make sense of it."

"So many people dream of doing what we do. It's tiring, though, and at my age, I can tell that my years of discovering are becoming numbered, but I'm happy there are young people like you willing to carry on the work."

Elisa grinned and leaned against Paoula's shoulder. "You're still young. You have years left yet."

"Maybe I'd have more if I'd landed a cushy job like yours." Paoula ragged her. "How about some lunch? You must be starving. You can tell me all about what Atef has you slaving over at the museum that's kept you away for so long."

Elisa laughed, "I only just started."

"Still. I want to know everything and...there's someone I'd like to introduce you to."

They had reached the opening of the corridor and they walked back up to the tent where a makeshift picnic had been set out.

Paoula approached the table and touched a man on the back of the shoulder. "Tomas," he turned around and embarrassment and terror flooded through Elisa. *Fuck.*

What's wrong, she heard Nef's startled question in her mind.

"This is Dr. Elisa Kent. Elisa, this is Tomas Williams, the archeologist I mentioned. This is his tenth season with us."

Elisa looked into the eyes of the one and only man she'd ever had a relationship with and felt like she'd been punched in the gut. He looked just as surprised to see her.

"Lisa!" He had a sandwich in one hand and a mouthful of food. He quickly swallowed it. "Hi. It's good to see you."

Paoula looked confused. "Do you two know each other?"

Elisa just stared at him, anger and hurt showing up on her features that she was having a hard time disguising. She reminded herself that she was a professional woman and curator of a museum now. This was the man who had taken three hours to identify the wrong language. She felt somewhat better at that and finally came back to herself.

"Tomas and I go way back. We attended university together."

Paoula seemed satisfied with this answer and invited Elisa to sit with them. She took some tea and a few finger sandwiches to give herself something to do other than stare at Tomas. Paoula was talking but Nef interrupted her in Elisa's thoughts.

Are you all right? Elisa could feel his presence behind her but didn't turn around.

I'm fine.

He didn't sound as easily convinced. *I think murder is frowned upon these days.*

I don't want to murder him, exactly.

Are you sure about that? I'm sure I could devise some clever spill off the side of the mountain. Maybe scare him into insanity.

Elisa chuckled and coughed to cover it up, pretending to be choking on her tea.

I don't like him, Nef almost snarled in her mind.

You don't even know him.

He hurt you. That's all I need to know.

Paoula was asking Elisa something directly, though what she had no idea. Paoula asked again and Elisa spent the rest of lunch avoiding Tomas's gaze as much as possible and telling Paoula what was going on at the GEM. She mentioned Nef, though not by name, and the mystery of her own mummy. Paoula seemed intrigued.

"We have some time after lunch. You should go over to Thutmose's tomb and see what you can find. Maybe something will spark."

Well, that was easy, Nef interrupted again.

Elisa really hoped she'd be able to take a nap in the shade of one of the extra tents after lunch, but her time here was short and Paoula's invitation was too good to pass up. She gathered the tools she thought she might need and told Paoula she'd be back within the hour.

As she walked up the hill to Thutmos' tomb, she felt Nef beside her.

"This is going better than I could have hoped."

She glanced up at him. He was smiling again. She was sure he'd never experienced Christmas, but couldn't help but think that this is what he might have looked like if he'd had a stack of presents sitting in front of him waiting to be opened.

"Don't get too excited, just yet. We still don't know what might be there, or not be there." While she'd intended to help him find what he needed, she suddenly wasn't sure she was ready to let him go.

Chapter Nine

Thutmose's tomb looked the same as she remembered it. KV-34, as the local archaeologists referred to it, was one of the most magnificently ornate tombs left in the Valley. Hieroglyphs adorned every wall. The outer chamber was spacious and well-lit for tourists. His wooden sarcophagus lay in the middle of a smaller room, intricately decorated with glyphs that were sure to make even the most magnanimous pharaoh jealous.

"So Tomas was the guy from college, right?"

"In the flesh." She was still trying to shake off the shock of seeing him. *I guess this was the job he left me for*, she thought. Ironic that now she was a museum curator and he was still working at dig sites. She tried not to feel too smug about that, but it took some of the sting out of seeing him.

Nef seemed to catch on to her mood. "Hopefully, I can take your mind off of him for at least a moment. I'd like to try to show you something. I've only done this once before, and, in all honesty, I don't know how it really works."

Elisa turned to look at him. He was giddy again. She had worried that being back here might make him sad, but he seemed more excited than anything.

Unsure what she was agreeing to, she nodded.

"Close your eyes and take a few deep breaths. Clear your mind." She consciously focused on her inhales and exhales. She could hear nothing in the tomb. Feel nothing except the hard stone beneath her feet and the buzz near her left arm that signified Nef's presence. That feeling reminded her of how his lips had felt on hers just that morning.

That's not clearing your mind, Elisa, came his voice in her head.

Embarrassed and flushed, she turned her attention to her breath again. In, out.

"Okay, now open your eyes."

In front of her stood people out of time working on a very empty and half-painted room. There were dozens of people working, hauling in stones, and even a few beginning to paint. Torches lit the ante-chamber and cast eerie shadows on the walls. She couldn't believe what she was seeing.

"What is this? How...how are you doing this?"

"I like to think of it as a projection. It's not real, of course. Only from my memory. The same way I can conjure clothing on myself at a whim and materialize in front of you. The *how* of all of it is a bit of a mystery to me, but if I concentrate hard enough, I can share my memory of what this place looked like when I was alive."

Elisa didn't know what to say or how to react. The images of everything were so clear. As soon as they had appeared, they were gone.

Bereft, she looked at Nef. He shook his head sadly. "It doesn't last long. Like anything else I have to do in the living world, it takes significant effort."

She could tell he was a little paler than he had been, though not as bad as when he'd tossed his finger at her.

"Thank you for showing me. That was...amazing."

He shrugged, "I wish I could show you more. Shall we continue on our quest?"

Elisa took in the room with a new appreciation. She had always appreciated it as an academic and a scholar, but now saw the human capital that had gone into creating such a space. A place where death was just as important—if not more so—as the life that was lived.

Nef walked slowly past her into the smaller chamber where the body of his friend had once been. In the middle of the room was an image of Thutmos. Nef stopped in front of it and mumbled something Elisa couldn't quite make out. When he turned back to her, his eyes were filled with emotion.

"It's an intriguing thing, isn't it?"

"What's that?" she asked softly.

"We prepared for death. Even welcomed the afterlife. We wanted to be remembered. We wanted our names to live on for eternity...and they have. They will. Not just because of our gods and goddesses that allow us to live in the beyond, but because of people like you who preserve our history. Our way of life is long since passed, but this…" he placed a transparent hand on the wall over Thutmos, "this remains."

Elisa smiled slightly, "We try, though it's not as important to some as it is to others." She thought fleetingly of the digs she'd been on that had to be stopped due to lack of funding. People now were more focused on the future than they were on the past. She moved next to Nef and examined the image of Thutmose III in all his royal regalia.

"History defines who we are, where we've been. Even where we're going. It's worth preserving. Remembering." Caught up in the spell of the past, she found herself getting choked up with emotion at her own history. She cleared her throat.

"Is this a good likeness of him?"

Nef glanced from her to the painting and smiled. "As much as it can be, yes. Though I prefer photographs now."

She turned and scanned the room. "So what is it I'm looking for exactly?"

"Ah, there should be an inscription somewhere. It's probably hidden, but his original plans were to have it built into the stone along the base of this room."

"Well, that's going to be a challenge, because they've built a wall here." A three-foot-high wall separated visitors from getting too close to the inscriptions and hieroglyphs painted everywhere.

She looked at the painting again. Thutmose was seated on a throne with a black base. It was curiously less ornate than the other parts of the wall. She leaned closer and turned her headlamp on. At the base of the throne was a standard script that warned would-be grave robbers of all of the horrible things that would happen to them if they took anything from the tomb.

Come for my soul, O you wardens of the sky! If you delay letting my soul see my corpse, you will find the eye of Horus standing up thus against you … The sacred barque will be joyful and the great god will proceed in peace when you allow this soul of mine to ascend vindicated to the gods… May it see my corpse, may it rest on my mummy, which will never be destroyed or perish, she translated.

"I'm impressed. It slips from your tongue so easily."

Elisa shrugged. "I've been reading varying forms of ancient Egyptian since I learned how to read."

Nef regarded her carefully and she grew uncomfortable in his gaze. She knew she probably shouldn't be touching the ancient wall, but a small square of sandstone that was painted black to blend into the throne caught her attention. It was almost hidden by the shape of one of the glyphs and she couldn't help but reach out to touch it. The small chunk of stone moved slightly when she rubbed her fingers over it, and she pushed a little harder.

Elisa glanced up at Nef as if asking permission to do what she was about to do. If anyone had actual rights to this tomb, it was definitely the 3,500-year-old ghost standing next to her and not the Egyptian government. He nodded at her.

With a little more effort, she pushed the stone in, and a large chunk of stone beneath it, the piece that made up the throne, moved. She held her breath as she took the ancient sandstone beneath her fingers and pulled.

Chapter Ten

"Well, that was disappointing." Elisa sat on the floor of the tomb with the giant stone in front of her. Behind it had been an empty space filled with what may have been papyrus at one time but had turned to dust. She could see a gap in the stones in the back that had probably allowed air and some amount of moisture to creep in. Either that or grave robbers had been more cunning than she'd ever given them credit for.

"If your heart and the scroll or anything belonging to Thutmos ever were in there, they certainly aren't now."

Nef sat on the floor beside her, looking sullen again. "At least we tried." He looked at her, sincerity etched on his features. "Thank you. I know it was a risk you didn't have to take, but thank you just the same."

All that was left was to try to fit the stone back in place before someone discovered that she had taken it out. Nef was no help with the lifting, but he was able to walk her through the mechanism of how it worked so she could slide it back in seamlessly.

"What other secrets do you know about these tombs? You might be handy to keep around." She wiped her dusty palms on her pants and smiled at him.

He chuckled a little at that. "It seems I'm not the only one who knows these secrets, so I'm not sure I'd be much help, but I do like being 'around,' as you say."

The look he'd given her in the bathroom was back. The one that made her feel tingly and alive.

Elisa couldn't help but glance at his lips. "I think we should probably get back. Paoula is going to send a search party soon."

They walked through the tomb and out into the darkening day of the Valley. The sunset here was almost as glorious as watching it set behind the pyramids. Elisa paused as they reached the opening of the tomb and looked over at Nef. "Do you miss it?"

He sighed and put his hands in his pockets, a very modern gesture, she noted.

"I miss the people. I don't miss the war, disease, and famine. I know they all exist today, but it's more manageable now than when I was living. It's terrible to watch children die of starvation when the rains stop. I don't miss that. Or the smell of death. There are many wonderful things about your time, and the life you live, though some of it feels very…primitive compared to the way we lived.

"All I've ever wanted since I realized I hadn't moved into the afterworld was to get there. To my family." He turned his face in the glow of the sunset to Elisa, "But now, I find I quite like it here with you."

Elisa blushed again. This was becoming a habit. One she couldn't wrap her head around. Only she would have a crush on a ghost. *Figures*, the thought, then chided herself for not censoring her thoughts better. Nef smiled and reached out to her. This time, he didn't stop himself from grazing his fingertips along her jawline. Elisa closed her eyes and leaned into what felt like a low electric buzz. She heard Nef's breath catch and opened her eyes to find him staring at her in wonder. His eyes had turned to pools of black again and all she wanted was to lose herself in them.

She startled at the sound of footprints coming up the slope toward her.

"Lisa?" Tomas, the last person on earth she wanted to see right now, walked up to her. "Paoula asked me to come get you. We're having dinner soon and then we'll all go over to the dig house together."

Elisa looked at him and tried not to scowl.

"Did you find what you were looking for?" He asked, professionally.

"Sadly, no." She shifted her backpack and started the walk back to the main tents.

Tomas walked beside her, clearly not acknowledging the distance she was trying to put between them. "Don't worry. We find things that have been moved from tomb to tomb all the time. Maybe whatever you're looking for about who this guy could be will turn up."

Elisa used every bit of strength she had not to roll her eyes at him, but said "Yeah, thanks Tomas," while she walked as fast as her petite body was capable of.

"Wait, Lisa," he called after her. She stopped but didn't turn around.

"Please don't call me that, Tomas. Dr. Kent will do."

"Right. I owe you an apology."

At that, she did turn to face him. She could feel the heat rising in her face and was powerless to stop the anger that was enveloping her. Her voice was calmer than she felt when she finally spoke. "Do you? Ten years later, Tomas?"

He had the good sense to at least look sheepish. "I know. I'm sorry. I was stupid. You were amazing. Clearly are still to get where you have." He reached out and touched her arm. Somewhere in her mind, Nef made a noise of dismay. She'd almost forgotten he was there.

"You deserved so much better than what I gave you. I'm sorry I left the way I did."

Elisa softened slightly at him but slowly shrugged her arm out of his reach.

"Thank you for the apology. I appreciate that." She turned and started to take a step when he called her back again.

"Hey, listen. Now that we're on speaking terms again, do you think you could let me know if anything opens up at the GEM? I'm starting to get tired of living in sand and dust most of the year."

This time she did roll her eyes. She kept her back to him as she made her way up the slope to dinner. "I'll keep an ear out."

Now can I scare him to death? Nef grumbled in her head.

Thank you, but no. Not tonight anyway.

Shame. I'll make myself scarce while you have dinner. Catch up with your friends.

That's not really necessary. Elisa glanced up at the tent with the dig team and noticed Paoula packing up for the day. She was laughing with her team.

It is, I think. You spend far too much time with the dead. Enjoy the living.

Where will you be?

Around.

Nef had either *poofed* or made himself disappear because Elisa could no longer see him. *He's like bloody Batman when he does that,* she rolled her eyes.

I am the night.

Elisa chuckled then tried to close her thoughts and made her way back to the tent.

Dinner at the dig house was uneventful, but Nef was right. She did need the company of the living. She hadn't talked much, but she listened to everyone around the table telling stories in Spanish or Arabic, or French or English. There was something fascinating about the way Egypt drew people from all other lands to her.

She was tempted to write a whole paper just on that, but she wasn't a sociologist so she'd leave that to them.

Elisa tossed her backpack at the foot of her bed. Ordinarily, she'd be sharing a room with someone, but Paoula mentioned at dinner that they were low on students right now. A fresh batch would be coming in next week, so she had the space to herself. The room wasn't much to speak of—two sets of bunk beds, two single beds, a nightstand for each with two large dressers on one wall, and a bathroom with two make-shift shower stalls, a sink, and toilet.

There was a small porch attached with a few chairs and a raised metal fire pit that someone must have smuggled in from somewhere.

Elisa had made herself a cup of mint tea and decided to drink it on the porch. There was no light pollution here, and a million stars blinked at her from above. She could imagine the ancient Egyptians doing their calculations for the pyramids with their guiding lights.

It also reminded her of her favorite poem, "The Blessed Damozel" by Dante Gabriel Rosetti. It was about a lover grieving on earth for his lady who was in heaven. She recited a few lines from memory,

> *The blessed damozel leaned out*
> *From the gold bar of Heaven;*
> *Her eyes were deeper than the depth*
> *Of waters stilled at even;*
> *She had three lilies in her hand,*
> *And the stars in her hair were seven.*

She chuckled to herself. The poem reminded her of a spirited debate that she'd gotten into with her cousin Theo about whether or not the poem had been at all inspired by Poe's "The Raven." He said no. Elisa insisted it had been. She bet him laundry for a week and trudged off to the Oxford library bright and early the next morning for proof.

She'd been so pleased to shove a book under Theo's nose later showing, in Rosetti's own hand, that she was right. Theo never bet against her again.

Another suiter I need to maim? Came Nef's deep rumble in her mind.

She smiled. *No. Never. I was just thinking about my cousin, Theo. You'd like him, I think. He's a professor. Very studious and academic.*

Nef sat down in the chair beside her.

Your memory felt tinged with sadness, though. Will you tell me why?

It was from a time when I was getting over my sadness. I was an angry teenager after I lost my parents. Theo...saved me in a way. He somehow helped make death more bearable. He introduced me to books that made it seem that way. Nothing more noble than death and the beloved. Even more noble if the beloved had died. Pining for everlasting love and all that. Elisa turned to look at him, not thinking about the fact that he had pined for his beloved while in limbo. That probably wasn't so romantic for him.

I'm sorry, she thought, *I...*

It's all right. It is a romantic notion.

Elisa finished the last sip of her tea.

I guess I'll get ready for bed.

I'll stay here and give you some privacy, though after this morning, seeing you naked is a sight I could never get enough of.

Elisa's blush was instant and she almost knocked over her tea cup trying to put it on the chair next to her.

You are a terrible flirt.

I'm an honest flirt.

There was nothing to do but ignore him. She got up and walked over to her backpack to retrieve her t-shirt and sleep shorts. She'd left the porch door partly open. It was unlike her, but she wondered if he'd peek his head in and watch her like he'd done this morning.

So you didn't mind me seeing you naked?

I didn't say that, she thought as she pulled her shirt over her head.

You should know, you have lovely breasts.

I bet you say that to all the ladies.

You're the only lady I've talked to in centuries.

Elisa laughed and bent over to pull her sleep shorts over her panties.

Your backside might be your finest asset, though.

She took her time pulling up her pants. She didn't see him in the room, but she assumed he was somewhere.

You are a terrible tease.

Elisa shrugged and tied her shorts at the waist. *I just figured you have few pleasures left being dead, so if watching me put clothes on makes you happy, it's the least I can do.*

I'd rather you took them off again.

I'm not that accommodating.

Nef huffed and appeared in the middle of the room while she got under the covers. Elisa glanced up at him from sleepy lids.

Shall I tell you a story to help you sleep?

Elissa nodded and yawned. It had been a long time since anyone had tucked her in, but she found she rather liked listening to him in her head or otherwise as she drifted. There was something so soothing about his voice. She wasn't sure what to make of this new, flirtatious dynamic between them, but she was enjoying his company too much to care.

The next few days passed by quickly. Elisa worked and Nef wandered around the Valley as much as he could. He talked to her every night as she got ready for bed and slept and she'd had dreams of the places he talked about. She missed him when he wasn't around during the day, but reminded herself that she should get used to it. She was trying to set him free and dwelling on her crush on him was going to get her nowhere but frustrated and brokenhearted.

Before long, she was done with her observations and had provided what she could with the translations. It was time to catch her flight back to Cairo. Part of her was glad to be going back—to have Nef to herself again—but conversations that she'd had with the dig team, even Tomas came to mind on her flight home. She realized how much she'd missed the camaraderie of people. She was used to being holed up in her basements and labs with her thoughts as her only company, but somehow Nef, Paoula, and Tomas had reminded her that her knowledge was valuable and should be shared more often. They didn't make her feel as awkward as she often felt. She could offer something more to her field. If she really wanted to make her parents proud, she'd have to come out from behind her lectures and papers and learn to interact with people again. She wouldn't get over her fear that people would just love her and leave her easily, but hiding had only left her lonely.

Until Nef had shown up.

They were both quiet as Elisa unlocked the door to her apartment. She'd been so lost in her thoughts that she didn't even remember telling the taxi driver where to go.

Bastet meowed at them from the sofa when they walked in and looked at them with eyes half-open.

"Ever the regal mother," Nef quipped.

Elisa smiled as she set down her keys and duffle. She felt the awkward tension that had been present in the Valley begin to snake around her belly. She'd have to talk to him.

"Listen," she started. At the same moment, he'd said her name and turned to her.

His smile was shy, which was something she'd never seen from him before. He was usually so confident—almost arrogant. She was supposed to be the one of the two of them that was unsure of themselves.

Her eyes widened a little when she smiled back, "You go ahead."

Nef played with the ring on his left finger—another uncharacteristic show of nerves. "I know how you feel about getting close to people. I know I can't change that," he squared his shoulders and put his hands in his pockets. When he looked her in the eyes, finally, Elisa could have melted. His deep brown eyes were full of an intensity that made them look like they were glowing. He looked down at his feet and cleared his throat.

"If we can't find my heart, I'd like to stay with you," he whispered. "It is selfish of me, I know. But I've felt more comfort and…happiness in these last few days of knowing you than I ever remember feeling when I was alive. Would you let me?" He looked back up at her, eyes searching.

"I…" Elisa wasn't sure what to say. Stay for how long? Until she met someone else? Until she died? Was he asking her to have a monogamous relationship with a ghost? She wanted him, but to never be able to touch him, or to feel his skin against hers would be torture. Her muscles clenched at the idea of him covering her body with his and making love to her.

She shifted and cleared her throat, hoping he hadn't heard that thought, but his eyes told her that he had.

He moved slowly closer to her, like a beast stalking its prey. His eyes had almost gone black and they were focused on her lips. A shiver of lust worked its way from her spine to the back of her neck. She licked her lips and let out a low groan. His hands came slowly out of his pockets and settled on either side of her jaw.

"Such pretty thoughts," he murmured close to her mouth. Her face tingled where he'd placed his hands and if she concentrated hard enough, she could almost feel what would be his breath against her lips. *But that's impossible*, she thought as she looked into his eyes. *All of this is impossible.*

"But it is not. Because I'm here with you now. And if you could only read *my* thoughts, you know that I long for the pleasure of your body in the same way you long for mine."

He brushed his lips against hers again, and this time, she expected the warm buzz and leaned into it. The tingling on her jaw moved to the back of her neck and she felt the lightest tug on the strands of her hair. She closed her eyes and imagined that he'd thread his fingers in her nape if he could.

Elisa's whole body warmed as the buzzing moved across her lips, onto her jaw, and down toward her neck. Pleasure coursed through her and desire settled firmly in her chest and stomach. She could feel the wetness growing between her legs as he tugged more firmly on her hair.

This must be hard for him to do, she thought, and her eyes flew open. *I'm making out with a ghost in my kitchen.* The thought was so preposterous that she couldn't help the giggle that escaped her.

"Don't," he said. "Don't think such things. For now, just let your thoughts be filled with me. With us. With what you feel."

Bastet chose that moment to jump off the sofa and weave between Nef's legs.

"If she can do that, then I must be here in some capacity, mustn't I?"

Elisa nodded. She wasn't fully convinced, but her body hadn't felt this alive in so long. She hesitated to want to let go of the feeling. She was tired of thinking. She wanted to just feel.

"I don't know how this is going to work, but...yes." She shook her head. "I don't really even know what I'm saying yes to, but yes."

Nef kissed her eyelid and she felt that warm tingle of his presence again. "I do not have all of the answers you seek, *Habiba*, but I have an idea to enjoy this moment."

When he pulled back slightly, Elisa felt a chill on her arms. She couldn't stop her brain from analyzing all of the ways this didn't make sense. He was non-corporeal. She shouldn't feel the temperature on her skin fluctuate when he wasn't close.

"I want to see you."

That stopped the thinking. Elisa chuckled to herself as she remembered the way Nef had looked at her coming out of the shower. His whole face had darkened with desire. Maybe he did actually want her.

Or she was the only woman he'd seen naked in centuries, so of course he'd desire her.

"Do you really believe that?" Nef reached up to tug gently at her hand and release her own hold on her body. He stepped close again to nuzzle her ear.

"It's logical."

"The way your mind works to talk you out of things that make you feel happy for the comfort of logic is maddening." His voice was a husky whisper in her ear.

"What do you *feel*, right now?"

"Scared."

"Tell me more. What does your body say? Not your mind."

Elisa closed her eyes and took stock of herself on a deep breath. Her breasts felt heavy, her heart raced, and she felt an intense desire to be touched. But really, she felt relaxed. Safe. Her shoulders weren't tense with anxiety. Her stomach wasn't rolling in anticipation of dread. She felt wanted, wholly and completely. As much as she could, she trusted Nef. He'd said so many times how much he appreciated her body and her mind. Maybe she could take him at his word.

Eyes still closed, Elisa tugged on the hem of her shirt and lifted it slowly over her head. She didn't feel Nef as close this time.

"Nef?"

"I just wanted to watch you for a minute."

Elisa lay back on the bed. The sheets felt cool under her skin, but her heart beat so rapidly she was afraid it was going to bounce her off. She closed her eyes and tried not to fidget. When she opened them again, Nef was still looking at her like *she* was a puzzle he wanted to solve.

"Now I know how my mummies must feel when I study them."

"I've been fortunate enough to be under your lingering gaze. I find I quite like it." He must have run a hand over her foot because Elisa felt a tingling vibration on her arch. It didn't tickle, but it startled her enough that she jerked away.

"Sorry," she blushed.

"Don't apologize."

"Will you talk to me while you touch me? It might help. It's been a while."

"I can feel your nervousness, ma cher. It's very loud too."

The sensation was back on the bottom of her foot. "You have such delicate feet, love. They're so soft. Do you like this?" The feeling moved up to both of her ankles, under the inside of the ankle bone. Heat and an ache began pooling deep in her belly.

"I didn't know I did, but yes."

"Your skin is so pale. If we were in my time, I'd place you on a table surrounded by fruits and feast on your body. I'd start here."

The fluttering on her skin moved up the backs of her legs to her calves.

"I would have my lips, my hands, everywhere all at once to satiate my desire for you. To taste you."

Desire coiled itself around her abdomen and between her legs. The feeling of him traveled up her body, and as it did, her nerves fell away. The chill of the air dissipated as Nef's energy blocked it from her skin. She looked down her lower body at him, his hands were on her thighs and he was bending to place his lips just over her belly button.

She normally liked to do all of this in the dark with her eyes closed, but watching him was like a drug she never wanted to stop taking.

She arched her hips, thinking how good that low buzz would feel between her legs. She didn't want this study of her body to end though. She'd never felt so worshiped by anyone.

Nef growled deep in his throat when Elisa reached her hands up to palm her own breasts.

"Does that feel good, love?"

She groaned as she watched Nef work his way further up her body. Warmth spread over her abdomen as his fingers traced circles from her hips to her stomach and back again.

"Move this hand for me and tell me if you feel this," he lowered his head to her nipple and kissed the hard tip gently then circled his tongue around it.

Sensation flooded her. It was almost like she'd placed a vibrator on herself, but there was no weight, which somehow made the pleasure more heady and more elusive.

"Yes, it feels wonderful," she said breathlessly.

He continued kissing around her nipple, then down the slope of her breast, across her sternum, and over to the other side.

"I want to try something. I want to show you how much I want you. What I'd do to you if I could."

Elisa's mind was clear of everything but him. She blinked, and the room was suddenly transformed into what she could only imagine was an ancient Egyptian bedroom. Nef was laying beside her, his fingers still circling her abdomen.

"Can you see it?"

She nodded.

She was momentarily distracted by wanting to study the room, in detail, but wasn't sure how long this *vision* would last.

"Don't worry, darling. I'm not going to let this go that easily."

In this vision, he slid his fingers into her hair. She somehow felt a gentle tug as if he really had. Her scalp tingled and she let out a moan.

Nef's mouth was on hers in what would have been a possessively punishing kiss if it had been real.

The desire she was feeling certainly was, though. His tongue clashed with hers in what an urgency to seek out everything she had to offer him. He palmed her breast himself and rolled his fingers over her nipple. Elisa did close her eyes, but the vision remained.

Nef was stretched out, tall, and lean next to her small, pale body while he torturously brought long-dead flames licking back to life. His fingers trailed down to her waist and across her hipbone.

"Did you know that your hips are one of my favorite parts of you to gaze on?"

She smiled against his lips and her hips lifted in invitation to him. This time, his fingers found her clit.

"Open for me, love."

Elisa opened her eyes again and her legs a little wider. She couldn't have known what his touch would feel like on her wet lips as he stroked her up and down, but it was better than she'd hoped for. Her hips rolled up and down to meet his strokes and he lovingly caressed her folds.

"You're so wet for me. So ready."

"Nef...I..." whatever she'd been about to say was cut off by the feeling of him slipping a finger inside her then easing out, then back in again.

She watched his vision of them and the feeling of him was enough to leave her panting for him.

Nef kissed her neck, then positioned himself on top of her. "You are a goddess to me, Elisa. If you only knew the power you have over me."

She could feel the buzzing, more intense at her entrance, then the vision of him slid so easily into her, and so slowly she dared not breathe. Torchlight lit his face as his eyes closed and he hung his head as he entered her again.

"Touch yourself for me, Elisa. Let me feel the pleasure in your mind."

Elisa's eyes felt heavy as she rolled her middle finger over the hard bud of her clit. Nef matched his thrusts in time to the rhythm of the circles she made. As her need increased, she could feel her lips begin to tingle and the muscles in her toes began to tighten as her orgasm threatened to spill over.

"Nef...please..."

"Find your pleasure, ma cher. I'm right here," He grunted as he pumped in and out faster and faster.

Elisa could see her vision body enraptured in pleasure and wrapping her legs tighter around him. She pinched her nipple in one hand while she picked up the pace on her clit with the other.

"That's it, love. Let go for me, Elisa." The way he moaned her name was enough for her.

She hadn't needed his permission, but as soon as he'd said it her orgasm crested over her like a wave that she had no choice but to ride. The muscles in her abdomen clenched and released and she let out a low moan while he pumped twice more then groaned himself as his vision-body emptied itself inside of her.

He held her for a while after, stroking her hair and watching her come back to her body.

"I thought your frustration was loud, but your orgasms are louder."

Elisa chuckled, "What do you mean? Did you *hear* that?"

"I don't have the words other than to tell you that it felt like joy and pleasure and happiness washed over me all at the same time. It was so warm. So full of light."

"That's just endorphins, adrenaline, and oxytocin."

"Ever my little scientist. Even in rapture." He smiled and lowered his forehead to hers. "Thank you for sharing yourself so completely with me. It is the ultimate gift."

She was quiet for a while. Then a thought occurred to her.

"Do ghosts get blue balls?"

He laughed so hard, she could have sworn the bed shook.

"Not as such. Ghosts don't get erections either but don't ever doubt how much I want you and how much absolute pleasure you give me.

"Sleep now, my love. I'll give you good dreams to guide you."

She closed her eyes and Nef gave her a vision of the Nile on a moonless, star-filled night. They were walking on the bank together, hand in hand, each carrying a clay lotus with a candle centered in the middle.

Chapter Eleven

Elisa was surprised to wake up alone the next morning. Her body felt like liquid after the events of the night before, but anxiety quickly replaced her peace. Getting dressed and showering took no time at all but the lump of worry in her chest grew larger.

He was probably just tired. That was a lot of energy to exert. She checked her bag to make sure Nef's finger was still in it before she walked out of the door. Downstairs, she hailed a cab and directed her driver to the GEM. The traffic in Cairo this morning didn't help her nerves.

When she finally made it into her lab, she made sure the door was firmly closed behind her before she said his name.

"Nef?" She heard the worry in her voice.

Here, she heard in her mind. *Just needed rest.*

His voice was so quiet in her mind, that she had to concentrate to hear it, but her heart finally slowed to a normal rhythm after she realized he was fine. Their experiment away from his body for so long and his mind-melding last night must have really cost him.

She took his mummified finger out of her bag and set it gently back in his wrappings with the rest of him.

Sorry I wasn't there when you woke up.

Elisa smiled. "It's okay," she said aloud. "That must have been difficult for you."

A little chuckle resonated in her brain. *It was worth it. I only wish I could have watched you sleep all night. I thought of you moaning for me instead. I hope we can do that again.*

Elisa heard the door handle click and immediately spun around to face Atef. She hoped she didn't look as guilty or flushed as she felt, but it took some effort to try to ensure her face wasn't flaming red.

"I heard you had a good trip," Atef smiled at her and walked forward to kiss her cheeks in greeting.

"I did, indeed."

"There's a present for you in your office." His eyes twinkled in some kind of mischief.

Elisa was momentarily confused and then realized the journals from her aunt must have arrived.

"After you're done up there, we have something you need to discuss. Can you meet me in my office around eleven?"

Elisa felt her brow furrow. She felt like she'd been asked to come to the principal's office. Maybe Atef found out she snuck part of a priceless artifact out.

"Mmmhmm." The pitch of her voice was about two octaves higher than usual.

"I'll go up with you," he smiled and gestured for her to walk in front of him out of her lab.

They chatted in the elevator about her discoveries in the tombs, and how impressed Paoula had been at how quickly she'd been able to translate and identify their mysterious woman.

"I knew hiring you was the right decision." They had already arrived at Elisa's office door and Atef nodded at her to enter. "Enjoy."

Elisa opened her office door expecting to find a package on her desk but instead found her best friend sitting on the sofa, texting away.

"Mir! What the hell are you doing here?"

They could not have been more different, but the two of them had bonded at Oxford. Miriam's mother had died not long before they started school and her father owned an architecture firm in New Orleans. She had run away to London chasing some guy and on daddy's money and her good French, she'd spent time all over Europe. These days, her interior design firm sent her all over the world to use her Southern charm—and her curves—on their clients.

The first time they'd met had been a Halloween party. Everyone on campus mistook Elisa for an Irishwoman because of her auburn hair, freckles, and tiny height. She decided to just embrace it and be a leprechaun as her costume. Some drunk bro had been picking on her when Miriam came in and saved the day. They'd been close ever since.

Miriam stood and wrapped her best friend in a fierce hug. "Oh, my favorite little leprechaun. How are you, honey?" Miriam leaned back and took Elisa by the shoulders. "Good, I think. You look like you finally got laid."

Elisa couldn't stop the heat from coming into her cheeks this time. She turned toward her desk to get out from under Miriam's scrutiny.

"Come on, woman. Spill. I want all the deets."

Elisa wasn't even sure what to say. Miriam's mother had been known to do Tarot readings and practice voodoo, and she knew Miriam was more open-minded than most because of that, but if she told Miriam the actual truth, she'd probably have her shipped back to London with a bed waiting at a mental hospital. Elisa knew she was a terrible liar, so she'd have to find a way to stick to the truth but bend it.

"Fine. I met someone, yes."

"And what does he do? Is he good enough for you?"

"He's...in antiques. He's fantastic. But I'm not sure it's going to last."

"It never does with you. You never let anyone get close enough, sugar."

"Hi pot, I'm kettle," Elisa smiled sweetly at her friend.

"Yes, well. Abandonment issues are a bitch aren't they?"

Miriam sat back down on the leather sofa, crossed her long legs, and threw her curls back over her shoulder.

"So what are you doing here?" Elisa sat back in her own chair.

"I'm not staying long. I'm headed back to London soon, but I thought I'd pop in and check on you. Also, I come bearing gifts."

Miriam bent down and retrieved an overnight shipping package from her bag.

"From Theo and Mae. Mae didn't have your address and Theo was shipping me something anyway, so I just had him include this in it. What is it?"

Elisa got up and retrieved the parcel while rolling her eyes. "I only emailed her my address like four times. What was Theo sending you?"

"Well, you know dear Aunt Mae. I needed some documents from my flat, so I asked him to get them while he was watering my plants."

Elisa sat on the edge of her desk in the way she'd seen Nef do so casually so many times before and her heart squeezed at the thought of him.

I haven't gone that far.

She tried to keep her balance as his voice in her head so suddenly surprised her.

"I don't know why you two don't just marry each other and get it over with," she said to Miriam to cover her rapid heartbeat.

"Because we'd kill each other within a month. We almost did."

"Miriam," Elisa said sternly while she tore open the package, "that was fifteen years ago." Two leather-bound journals slid out of the packaging and into Elisa's hands. She couldn't hope too much that these would hold the key, but maybe they would point her in the right direction.

"Yeah, well, he hasn't changed much in that time, truth be told. What are those?"

"My great-grandfather's journals. It turns out I'm working on something he also worked on back in 1903. I'm hoping this will help me with something."

"I love how excited you get about your mystery mummies, but I know that look. You have determination and work, blah, written all over you."

"Again, hi pot. You work more than I do."

Miriam leaned back in on the sofa and spread her arms over the back. "But at least what I get to do is fun. Creativity and money and clients and actually getting to meet people."

"And using that big brain of yours to get men in particular to do whatever you want?"

Miriam smiled at her. "That too. And the boobs don't hurt either. When can I pull you away from work? I'd love to take you to lunch or dinner before I leave."

Elisa set the journals on her desk.

"I can make time tonight. I'm not in a hurry to start on these."

"Hear, hear. The dead can wait, right?"

"They can, but the living can't. I have a meeting with my boss in a few minutes. Where are you staying? I'll come meet you, or we can meet at my apartment."

"The Ritz, darling. Where else would I be?"

Elisa chuckled. "Why did I even ask?"

"Do you end work at five like normal people?"

"Not lately, but I think I can make an exception for you."

"Why did I even ask?" Miriam smiled and got up to walk over to Elisa, then grabbed her hands. "I wish I could stay longer. I hate that I only get to see you about once a year."

Elisa reached up to hug her. In heels, Miriam was almost a foot taller than she was, "I know. Me too. But we video chat all the time when you aren't traveling all the time."

"Well, hopefully, that's about to end soon," Miriam pulled back. "I'm hoping to be able to stay in the home office for a little while when I get back. And then I think Daddy wants me to pay him a visit. You should come."

"To New Orleans? I'd melt. You should stay in London and marry my cousin."

"Pushy, pushy."

Elisa felt a tingle in the air and when she turned to look over nonchalantly over her shoulder, Nef was sitting in her chair. He was paler than normal, but at least he was slightly visible.

Don't scare her, please.

He looked appalled. "Me? I would never."

Elisa startled at him speaking out loud but quickly remembered Miriam couldn't hear him.

"You okay, honey? You look a little pale all of a sudden."

"Yeah, fine."

"I bet you forgot to eat again today. You can't just live on coffee, El."

"I know, you're right. I know better," that would have to cover her. "I promise to eat as soon as my meeting is done."

"Good. All right. I'll let you get back to work." Miriam looked over Elisa's shoulder. "Great view, by the way. We should take a selfie and send it to Mae. She'll have a million questions for me when I get back. She won't believe you're alive unless I show her proof."

Miriam got out her phone, and the two women smiled for the camera with the pyramids of Giza on display in the background.

"Huh, it's chilly over here. That's odd, with so much solar gain and these windows, it should be warmer."

Elisa changed the subject. "Will you send that to me?"

Miriam looked at her phone. "Sure. That's odd. It's a little blurry in the background. Look, right where your chair is."

Elisa panicked. She looked at the phone display. Miriam was right. Fortunately, there was nothing to distinguish a face or body in the photo. She glanced at Nef.

"How odd. Must just be a weird reflection on the glass."

Nef got up and moved across the office to lean against the bookcase. "Let's try another one."

Miriam held up the phone again and snapped another shot. "Much better. I'd say your office is haunted, but all of this is too new, right?" Miram winked at her. "All right. Text me when you leave. We can meet in the hotel bar and then I'll take you out somewhere."

"Sounds good, but not too late. It is only Monday."

"Yes, ma'am," Miriam kissed her on the cheek and walked out singing a cheery "see you later," as she sashayed away.

Elisa rounded on Nef. She should be used to him barging in by now, but it still unsettled her when he chose to show up around other living people.

"Now? You had to come up now?"

"I missed you." He walked over to her and touched his finger to her lips. "Don't pout. Plus, I wanted to meet Miriam. You were thinking such loving thoughts about her, I didn't want to wait."

"Isn't she great? I think I'm glad you didn't meet her first. Most men don't even see me when we walk into a room together."

"I suppose she is beautiful, by modern standards, but she isn't you."

Nef leaned closer to place his lips gently on Elisa's. She felt the warm tingle on her own lips. It would have been so easy to get lost in him again, but her phone chimed to remind her she only had five minutes until she met with Atef.

"You're still a little pale. You should get some more rest. I have a meeting, but I'll be down when I'm done."

Nef leaned his forehead against Elisa's. "Don't be long. And don't forget to eat, little liar." And then he was gone.

Elisa walked into Nef's office a minute early. He was finishing up a call, but he motioned to one of the chairs facing his desk. His office looked much the same as hers, but every conceivable surface was covered with some kind of artifact, framed papyrus, or dig photo. His desk was the only space that was mostly clear of items, though there were stacks of papers meticulously organized on all four corners.

He hung up the phone and smiled at Elisa. "I have good news. That was the Metropolitan Museum in New York. They're going to be putting some of our items on display and your new mummy is going to be the centerpiece of the collection."

Elisa's heart dropped into her stomach and it quivered like she might be sick.

"But I haven't identified him yet, Atef."

He waved her off. "They don't much care about that. I've been working on this with them for what feels like ages. You've done such excellent work cataloging in such a short amount of time, that they've agreed to a five-year loan, and then a US tour to other museums after that for another five years."

Elisa knew what this meant for Atef and the GEM. Having ancient artifacts on display in America would only enhance the optics of the museum here and create contacts in other museums that Atef surely needed. The creation of the GEM hadn't been cheap, and museum patrons only paid so much. A ten-year contract for one of the most complete sarcophagi and funerary ephemera in recent memory would be a feather in his cap to the Board for a long time.

"I haven't finished everything just yet. When is this happening?"

"Do you think you and Robert could have everything done by next week? They'd like to start making plans and have everything packaged and shipped to them as soon as possible. We've created an immersive section to go along with everything."

"I wish you would have told me this when you brought me on. I didn't know I was working under a deadline."

"I'm sorry, Elisa, I didn't know that would affect you. In all honesty, I didn't even know that you'd be able to sustain work in the lab after we had so many people leave. I've been working on this for a long time and after I saw the progress you were making, I told them we could move forward. Robert told me he finished some sections while you were at the dig. I thought you'd be excited that your first real mummy would be on exhibit."

Atef was confused by her reaction. This was the goal of most Egyptologists—to share their finds with the world so that the history of this culture wasn't lost or forgotten. Before meeting Nef, Elisa would have been elated to hear this news.

Nef. How was she going to tell him? She knew it had been a bad idea to get involved with him in any way, but now he was leaving her. Granted, it wasn't his choice to leave her, but the result was the same, nonetheless.

Elisa tried to cover her reaction and turn her brain off at the same time so Nef wouldn't appear in her office. She couldn't face him right now.

"You're right, Atef. I am excited. I just would have loved to know who he was before I shipped him off for a decade."

Atef visibly relaxed. "I know. You must not like leaving work unfinished. You have a reputation for being a sort of...mummy detective. I wouldn't have expected anything else from you, but this has been a big find for us, and it's time we share him with the world. It took me a long time to get the government on board, so I don't want to diminish their goodwill."

"I understand," Elisa looked at her hands and clasped them tightly together. "How long do we have?"

"The whole collection needs to be ready to leave by Friday. Robert mentioned while you were gone, that you've cataloged about 95% of the collection. I trust you'll be able to finish by Thursday, but just in case, I'm bringing in some extra hands."

"Which brings me to my second piece of news. Paoula recommended someone you know. She said you worked well together at the dig site." Atef referred back to his notes. "A Tomas Williams?"

Elisa's nausea was back.

"He'll be here later today to get settled in."

Elisa forced a grin but was sure it looked more like a grimace. "Perfect." She needed to get out of here for a while. The air suddenly felt too close.

"Actually, I got my great-grandfather's journals this morning. My friend dropped them off. Do you mind if I take the rest of the day at home to review them? It's quieter there. He worked on this sarcophagus back when it was initially discovered so I thought he might have some insight."

"Of course. If that's what you need. I think Robert can show Tomas around until you're back tomorrow. Here's to hoping you find something."

Elisa nodded and excused herself from Atef's office. She made her way back to her own and gathered the journals and her keys. Her work bag was downstairs, but she didn't want to trek down there now and risk Nef cornering her. She tried to think of anything else that wasn't related to the conversation she'd just had in case Nef "heard" her thinking and settled on re-alphabetizing her books in her head.

When she was finally home, Bastet weaved herself between Elisa's legs. Unable to keep the idea of losing Nef at bay, she sat on the floor and let her emotions catch up to her brain. Bastet jumped in her lap and licked a tear from her nose.

"What am I going to do, little mother?"

Bastet purred and butted her head against Elisa's forehead. It seemed she didn't have any answers either.

Chapter Twelve

Several hours later, Elisa hadn't found anything helpful in Charles Kent's journals. She understood why Aunt Mae may have thought he was mad. There were notes about talking to an "invisible friend." Charles had apparently even contacted a spiritualist and a priest, unbeknownst to Nef, to send him back to the afterworld, but to no avail.

In the years he had gotten to know Nef, he had documented their path of trying to communicate with one another. Charles even wrote out some words in phonetic Ancient Egyptian and what he thought their English equivalent might have been. It seemed more like another puzzle for her to solve, but it wasn't one she had time for right now.

There was no information about another dig in the area at the time or anything else that might have been found in the tomb. The GEM had the original itemized list from 1903 that documented all of the funerary objects and findings and it seemed to match up with Charles' account in his journal.

Elisa almost threw the journal at the wall in frustration but decided to message Miriam instead.

Done early. Rough day. Need a drink.

Miriam didn't hesitate to respond this time.

First round's on me. I'll meet you downstairs in 20.

Elisa didn't even have the energy to change clothes to meet Miriam in the posh hotel lobby. She was still too raw from Atef's news and the disappointment of finding yet another dead end. Logically, she knew that this was often the way of things in her line of work; not every mystery could yield answers, but her heart had gotten involved this time. She knew it'd be a dangerous undertaking, but something like hope had blossomed with Nef and she'd hoped they'd at least have more time together. Now all of that time she'd hoped for would be condensed to three days.

When she arrived at the opulent bar nestled in the back of the lobby at the Ritz, Miriam was already seated on a bar stool with a martini in front of her and a gin and tonic with a twist of lime sat aligned with the empty seat next to her.

She patted the white leather as Elisa approached. Without even sitting, Elisa downed the entire gin and tonic in only a few gulps.

"Wow. Wanna talk about it?" Miriam motioned to the bartender to ask for another in flawless Arabic.

Elisa sat down and slumped forward. Where did she even begin?

"First of all, the guy? He's...leaving."

Miriam sighed. "I'm so sorry, honey. Did you not know?"

"No. He didn't know. It's only been a week, but I feel more connected to him than to anyone else I've known," she glanced at Miriam. "No offense."

"None taken. Is he coming back soon? Maybe you can just do long distance."

Elisa took a slower sip of the fresh drink that had just been set in front of her. "It's...a ten-year assignment. In New York."

"Fuck me. That's a long time to be apart, but New York isn't *that* far. And it is mostly civilized. They do have internet maybe you can just—"

"You and I both know that long distance never works. Even if I visit him." There was so much more Elisa wanted to elaborate on, but she couldn't.

"Have you talked to him about all of this?"

Elisa put her head on her arms. "No."

"So, what? You found out and just...ran?"

"Pretty much."

"Jesus Christ on a cracker, El. Look, I'm not one to lecture anyone on relationships, but don't you think you should at least try to talk to him about this? I hear communication is all the rage in normal, productive, adult relationships."

"But it won't change anything, will it?"

Miriam rubbed her back. "I don't know. It might. It might be helpful to at least know what he wants."

"Maybe. I don't know."

"You really like this guy, yeah? I could see it written all over your face this morning. And clearly you've slept with him, which I know you don't do easily, so something in you must trust him. Trust him to be able to talk to you."

"I can't explain it. But it's...he's in my head. It's like he's the first person to *see* me. Really see me and try to understand me. I didn't think it was possible for me to feel this way about someone after such a short amount of time. It doesn't make any logical sense."

"Darling. Love—and lust—don't follow logic. Sometimes it's okay to just listen to your heart. And yes, that often leads to hurt, but it's better to have that than nothing, isn't it?"

"Right now, I would say no. I should have known better. Love just...hurts."

"But it's that hurt after the love that makes us feel alive. It's knowing that we exist and can love again that makes it all worth it, right?"

"Ask me in a month."

Elisa took another sip of her drink. Even after being reminded, she still hadn't eaten today, and the gin was already starting to make her feel a little tipsy.

"To make matters worse," she held up a finger, "one, the project I'm working on isn't done and it's being shipped out from under me. Two," she held up another finger, "You remember Tomas?"

Miriam sipped her drink. "How could I ever forget?"

"Well. I ran into him at a dig last week, and my boss just informed me that he's going to be working for me for at least the rest of the week...if not longer."

"Well piss on that."

"Exactly."

"Personally, I would find every way to make his life a living hell, but I know you're not me. So what are you going to do?"

"Stay as far away from him as I possibly can. It's not like I have a choice, but I can give him menial tasks that hopefully keep him out of my hair for a while."

"I know this isn't what you want to hear, but you can always come home."

"You mean quit?" Elisa sat up and looked at Miriam like she'd just slapped her across the face. "I just started! This is the only job I've ever really wanted. I can't just leave."

Miriam smiled. "That's what I was hoping you'd say. So, buck up. Get drunk tonight. Start fresh in the morning. If there's anyone I know who can overcome these minor hurdles, it's you. Do what you always do: solve the puzzle. Organize things. Find the patterns, ignore the people."

Elisa raised her glass and waited for Miriam to do the same. "Cheers to that."

"Now, let's feed you before you puke on my Louboutin's."

A few hours later, a little worse for wear, Elisa hung on Miriam as she got her up to her apartment. She'd eaten, but the alcohol she'd consumed with dinner had tipped her over the edge into blissfully forgetting what she'd been upset about in the first place.

She was humming something off-key while Miriam got her water and searched her cabinets for a pain killer. When she found what she was looking for, she handed them to Elisa.

"Drink up. You're going to regret all of this in the morning."

"Probably."

Elisa dutifully swallowed the water and pills while Miriam sat next to her.

"Do you want me to put you in bed, or are you happy on the couch?"

Elisa buried her head in one of the pillows. Somehow, it smelled like Nef. Frankincense and musk filled her nostrils as she took a deep breath in.

"I'll die here, thankyouverymuch."

"As you wish." Miriam kissed the top of Elisa's head. "I'm heading back. My flight leaves early tomorrow."

"I wish you could stay."

"I know, honey. But I'll come back and you'll come home for a visit before too long, yeah?"

"Probably in June." Elisa stretched her legs out on the sofa. "Thanks for listening. And for being a good friend and getting me drunk."

"You did that yourself, but you're welcome. Sleep tight, little leprechaun. Love you. Text me in the morning if you remember."

Elisa threw her arm over her eyes and closed them. "Yep."

She was beginning to drift off as the door closed behind Miriam, but Bastet came out of the guest bedroom and sat on top of the coffee table where Elisa had placed Charles Kent's journals. She meowed at Elisa.

"I don't want to feed you right now. Can you wait until morning?"

Bastet meowed again, then started batting the journals off the table. The first one landed with a *thud* on the tile floor. Elisa looked over at her just as she knocked the second one to the floor.

"What was that for?" Elisa sat up too quickly to pick them up and wobbled. Her vision swam as she bent down to pick them up. Sticking out of the cover of the second journal was a photograph.

Elisa ignored the journals and reached for it. It was a photograph of Charles Kent standing in the middle of Nef's tomb. Behind him was a low wall that served as a shelf for several objects, a few of which were the canopic jars that held his vital organs. Elisa counted. She knew there would be four, but this photograph showed her there were five. She counted again while she made her eyes focus.

She picked up the first journal that had contained Kent's itemized list of what had been found in the tomb. Four jars were listed.

Elisa examined the photo again. The jars were the standard of the era and depicted the four sons of Horus: Hapi the baboon protected the lungs, Qebehnsenuf the falcon guarded the intestines, Duamatef the jackal guarded the stomach, and Imsety the human guarded the liver. But the last jar depicted the head of a woman with cow horns on her head.

"Hathor. Goddess of love…and the heart. I'll be damned, Bastet."

Chapter Thirteen

Elisa didn't want to go to work the next day. Not only because she had a monster hangover, but also because she didn't want to face Nef or Tomas. It was true she might have some kind of a lead, but the canopic jar with Hathor had gone missing some time between the photo being taken and the items being cataloged. There were any number of places in the world where that canopic jar could be. The only thing she knew was that her lab wasn't one of them.

It would, however, be hard for someone to miss a canopic jar with Hathor on top, because as far as she knew, it was the only one of its kind. She needed access to the GEM's archival database and for that, she would have to go into the office. And deal with people.

She groaned as she sat up and trudged to the kitchen for water and more pain relief. Bastet meowed at her and wove between her legs the whole time she was in the kitchen.

"Didn't you used to feed yourself before you came here?"

In answer, Bastet turned around and sat on both of Elisa's feet.

"I definitely can't feed you if you sit there." Elisa picked her up and held her like a baby. Bastet purred and licked her nose.

"I guess I can't be too mad at you." Elisa glanced at the photograph sitting on the coffee table. "Were you a detective in another life, little mother?"

Bastet purred louder and closed her eyes while Elisa rubbed her stomach.

"You know, we could pretend like I didn't find this. I don't have to tell Nef or anyone. It's not going to matter anyway, because I'm quite literally looking for a needle in a haystack."

Bastet stopped purring and chuffed at Elisa.

"I know," she sighed. "Nef's just going to read my thoughts when I get there anyway."

Elisa put Bastet down and opened a new can of cat food and poured it on what she'd come to think of as Bastet's plate.

The cat devoured the fish-flavored pate, making happy eating noises all the while.

"Right. Solve the puzzle. Ignore the people, easy." Bastet looked at her with what might have been a cat-scowl.

"Don't look at me like that. You're a cat. Your job is to disdain people."

She searched through the cabinets for something edible and begrudgingly ate something herself, even though she felt a little queasy still, then showered. She practiced the conversation she'd have to have with Nef while she washed her hair and brushed her teeth. She would have to be stoic. There was no room for emotion now that he was leaving. She would do what she could to try to find this jar before he left, but after that, she'd have to move on with her work and her life.

Just the thought made a hole open up in her middle. She wouldn't have minded if it swallowed her whole.

It was still early when Elisa arrived at the GEM. No tourists were wandering the hallways just yet. This was her favorite way to be among the ancient artifacts that had been in the hands of only a few people like her. She glanced up at "her" Tut at the entrance. He towered over her as he always did, looking regal and powerful.

She passed a relief of Ra on her way to the elevator. She'd never been a particularly religious or spiritual person. The dig sites were her sanctuary and the ancient tomes her guides, but she couldn't help herself as she offered a silent prayer to the God of All.

"If there were ever a time I needed your guidance, it would be now." Her voice didn't raise above a whisper, but it still echoed back to her in the empty museum.

She thought she knew what she'd be met with when she entered her lab. She'd prepared herself for Nef to be angry with her, to demand answers for why she never returned yesterday. So she took a deep breath when her keypad beeped to allow her entry to the room and pushed open the door.

Nef was nowhere to be found. His sarcophagus was exactly where she left it. Nothing really looked like it had been touched since last week, though she could tell Robert had been busy cataloging more items into the database.

Her work bag

oto out of the front cover of the journal and set it up next to her keyboard. For a few minutes, she tapped the keys, searching through the GEMs database for any hint of irregular canopic jars. There were still thousands of items in the archives that had yet to be photographed, digitized, and updated from the old systems, but this had been moved to a cubby next to her computer, out of the way.

She pulled the ph was the easiest place to start to rule out places it couldn't be.

Photo after photo of hundreds of broken canopic jars flashed across her screen, but none with the head of Hathor. She couldn't have been sure that any of them *weren't* Nef's jar, but none were decidedly it either. Some weren't from the right period, so those were easy to rule out. She couldn't discount ones that had been broken, found with no lid, or found outside of the Valley of the Kings; it was possible a worker took this jar and it had ended up in another location.

After two hours of quiet searching, she felt more hopeless than she had at the start of this quest. She couldn't tell that she'd made any progress at all.

"What are you looking for?"

She'd been so focused on her search that she hadn't felt Nef appear behind her.

Now, the hairs on the back of her neck stood up, but she didn't turn away from her screen. She'd have to tell him sooner or later anyway before her loud thoughts betrayed her.

"A jar."

She felt him move closer.

"Lucky for you, there are several in this museum. Anything in particular? Maybe I can help. I do know this place quite well."

"Seen anything like this?"

She held up the photo behind her but still didn't face him.

"I don't understand. That's my tomb, yes?"

"Look at the jars..."

Nef leaned closer and Elisa could feel the air around her get warmer. "There are...five?"

"Yep."

Nef was quiet for a few minutes while Elisa began searching through journals and academic articles. Maybe the jar had found a home somewhere else.

"Elisa?"

She ignored him.

"Elisa. Please? Look at me."

She still didn't want to turn around. He didn't sound mad. She could deal with his anger because then she could be angry right back at him and the cruelness of the world that had brought them together only to separate them. But she couldn't deal with his sadness.

You don't have to talk to me. Would you rather I read your mind?

"No." He'd see and know everything that way, and she wanted to give him this information on her terms.

She sat up straight and squared her shoulders. As she pushed back from the table and started to turn around, Tomas and Robert walked into the room, chatting together and smiling.

"Good morning, Dr. Kent. Glad to have you back," Robert said cheerily.

Tomas glanced at Elisa then nodded. "Good to see you again, Li–Dr. Kent."

Fuck. "Good morning," She tried a smile but couldn't. "Robert, can you fill me in on the progress you made while I was gone? I want to be sure we're ready for Friday."

What's Friday? Nef's voice rang in her head.

She shook him off and tried to pay attention to what Robert was saying. He'd made a big dent in everything that had been found in Nef's tomb. Tomas even filled in here and there. Cataloging was menial, intern work, but his notes and process were efficient and they'd done well as a team yesterday.

Elisa. What is happening? Now Nef was starting to sound angry. She couldn't really blame him. He was respecting her request to not pry into her mind, though part of her wished he would, so she could just get it over with.

"Good work, both of you. Robert, if you can finish up those last three items of jewelry, I think we'll be set. Tomas, you can start packing items. We're fortunate that there are only about forty items in this whole collection.

"Atef sent me an email this morning. Everything is ready. There's a team coming in to help with moving the smaller items into crates at two today. They'll largely be here in the evenings so we don't get in their way and vice versa. Most of the packing items are in a room down the hall. I think you'll find everything you need in there. I'll help you with that after we take Ne–" Elisa barely caught herself, "our mystery man here to be x-rayed in the big machine and photographed. I'm on my way there in a few minutes."

She scanned the room and put her hands on her hips. "We'll have to work quickly, but I think we'll be able to get all of this done on time."

Packing? Elisa! Her work bag flew across the room and landed with a thump at her feet.

Tomas and Robert, both pale, looked at each other and then at her. She bent over and retrieved it calmly.

"How odd. Must have slipped." She brushed the bag off and turned around to put it back in place.

If you don't tell me what's happening, I'm going to start knocking all of these precious artifacts off the shelves.

Stop it, she screamed in her head. *I'll meet you in my office.*

She turned back to Robert and Tomas, "I have a few minutes before they come to wheel him into x-ray. I'm going to grab a coffee. Anyone want anything?"

They shook their heads but remained silent.

The elevator ride up to her office was the shortest she'd ever taken. *Stick to the facts. Facts are friends. Emotions are unruly monsters. Stick to the facts. Facts are friends.*

Nef was pacing back and forth in front of the window when she walked in.

When he stopped to look at her, his brow was furrowed and she remembered how intimidating and beautiful he'd looked the first time she'd met him. He'd told her he was a skilled killer and based on the way he looked now, she didn't have to work too hard to imagine what he looked like in battle. She felt her own frustration welling up inside her and was preparing to do a battle with him of her own.

I love him. I can't lose him. The thought came to her without any reason. He stopped and his face softened. He must have heard that one particular thought, otherwise he'd still be looking like he wanted to commit murder.

Her eyes misted and he walked slowly toward her. His fingers gently caressed her cheek and she felt that familiar energetic hum of his.

"You left me yesterday."

She looked down at her fingers. "I know. I'm sorry."

"You still looked beautiful this morning, even though you were ignoring me and clearly had a headache."

Elisa looked up into his face, expecting him to reveal he'd been listening in on her thoughts.

Instead, he touched her temple and rubbed. "You were pressing here, like it hurt."

"I, um, drank too much with Miriam last night."

"Ah."

Elisa moved away from him and this time, she began to pace.

"Why do you count your steps?"

She paused, mid-stride. "It's a self-soothing technique when I'm stressed. Most of the time I don't even realize I'm doing it." She held her hands up in a helpless gesture and then let them fall to her sides.

She didn't want it, but a gin and tonic would certainly make this conversation go down easier right now.

"I thought you weren't listening."

"You were yelling in your mind again. Why are facts friends?"

Elisa shrugged and sat down on the couch. Nef sat next to her and placed his hands over hers. Her body warmed immediately at the contact.

"Tell me, ma cher. Whatever puzzle has you so troubled, we can solve it together."

She took a deep breath and shoved her hair behind her ears. "The good news," she attempted a smile, "is that in my great-grandfather's journals, I found that picture I showed you. As far as I know, there have only ever been four canopic jars in any mummification ritual. Yours has five. The fact that Hathor is the figure on the top of the last one isn't an accident. The historical importance of that alone would be fodder for academic journals and lectures the world over. Four complete canopic jars are something of a revelation when we can find them whole like yours were, but five?"

"Elisa. Get to the point."

"Right. Well, the jar is in the photo and I'm reasonably certain that's where your heart is…"

"But?"

"I have no idea where it's gone. It wasn't in the records my great-grandfather made, and it's not in the records here at the GEM. It's like it just disappeared. And considering the fact that your tomb was discovered over 130 years ago and everything has been moved at least twice since then, there's no telling where it could be."

"That…doesn't sound like good news."

"I suppose it isn't, but at least we know it's in something unique."

"You haven't gotten to the part about packing."

The part Elisa was dreading. She got up and walked over to the window. The pyramids, aged as they were, stood gloriously where they'd been for generations. She'd always admired the mystery of them, and struggled with the inhumanity of the slavery, death, and heartbreak that had occurred as part of their creation. The Egyptians believed in balance above all else, and she realized as they beckoned her in the afternoon sun that just existing required the same. The good had to come with the bad. Maybe she and Nef could weather the next few years in the same way the mighty pyramids had.

She wrapped her arms around her body. "Atef has made a deal with a museum in New York. You're going to be put on display at the Metropolitan Museum for five years and then on an American tour after that for another five."

Chapter Fourteen

"You can't be serious."

Elisa couldn't face him.

"You leave in three days." Her breath fogged the glass of the window in front of her. She turned her head slightly. Enough that she could see Nef stand and run his fingers through his hair in a very modern and annoyed gesture. Elisa almost laughed. His gestures, at least, were adaptable.

"Look at it this way, I can spend time looking for that jar and hopefully your heart. It's only five years."

Atef started spewing curses in a language Elisa didn't understand. She'd never heard him speak his native tongue before and it sounded so foreign to her that she couldn't make heads or tails of it. But she knew he wasn't happy. In a better moment, she'd ask him to teach her.

"And as you just said, I've been awake for over 130 years, Elisa. No. No! You were supposed to be the one. I never would have brought you here–"

Elisa cut him off. "Brought me here?"

Nef looked at her but for the first time, she didn't feel like he saw her anymore.

"You didn't think you were the only qualified Egyptologist for this job, did you?"

"What are you saying?"

"I'm saying, I made sure you were the only one Atef would hire. You're of Charles' line. If anyone could free me from this cursed life it should have been you since he certainly couldn't."

Heat bubbled in Elisa's chest. This time, she wanted to grab the nearest object and throw it at Nef. She would have, too, if it wouldn't have just passed right through him.

That meant…she hadn't been brought here on her own merit. Nef had orchestrated the whole thing?

I Googled you. His words from the first day they met slammed into her memory.

Anger made hot tears appear under her vision. "They can't send you off soon enough. Get out."

"Elisa…"

"Out!"

He cursed a few more times and then disappeared.

Elisa channeled all of her energy and frustration and worked furiously for the rest of the day. She wasn't as gentle with Nef's objects as she should have been, and she stormed around the lab and in between Robert and Tomas while they worked silently around her.

At some point during the afternoon, she saw Robert shrug to Tomas and he leaned over to him and whispered, "She's not great with people."

I might not be, but my hearing works just fine, and I'm your superior.

The living and the dead could all go to hell as far as she was concerned. The end of the day couldn't come fast enough for her to escape this particular level of purgatory.

All she wanted to do was curl up in front of bad television and eat her weight in ice cream. Maybe for the rest of eternity.

When the workers arrived to begin packing everything up, she directed them what to take to the crates first and then stayed out of their way. Usually, she would have delighted in helping and making sure everyone was doing what they should be, but today she couldn't be bothered to care. They could shatter everything related to Nef and she wouldn't bat an eye.

When the time finally came for her to leave, she mumbled a brief goodnight to Robert and Tomas, threw her bag over her shoulder, and thought briefly about never coming back.

The cab ride took forever, but after her apartment door slammed behind her, she collapsed on the couch. She had too many emotions bubbling to settle on just one, so she threw a pillow across the room but that did nothing to alleviate the pressure in her chest. Hurt, betrayed, and confused by the one person she'd been convinced had really understood her. But none of it was real. He only understood her because he could read her thoughts. She was only here because he'd made it so. Not because she was good at her job. Not because she'd made strides in her field. Because Nef had wanted something, and like a careless boy, had done whatever it took to make that happen.

"Elisa?"

Startled, she sat straight up to see Nef looking at her from the kitchen.

"What the hell are you doing here?"

"We need to talk."

"How are you here?"

He glanced at her work bag on the floor of the kitchen.

"I snuck my finger into your bag when no one was looking."

"You're a conniving, manipulative bastard, and you need to leave."

Nef crossed his arms and looked down at her. "No."

Bastet entered the room from behind him and rubbed her side against his legs. After she'd done a complete circle, she stretched and yawned and lay on his feet.

"See? She agrees with me. I'm not leaving."

Elisa's face and chest were burning in embarrassment and anger, "What could you possibly have to say to me?"

Nef moved closer to the couch and knelt in front of her.

"I think you misunderstood me earlier."

"You made sure I was the one hired. You manipulated Atef and me. What is there to misunderstand?"

"I was angry. It may have sounded that way, but my intentions were...pure, I promise you."

"You're intentions were selfish. You used me."

"What would you have me do?" He walked across to the other side of the living room. "I've been a prisoner in a world I don't understand, watching it pass me by for so long. I woke up and everything was different. The world did not move the same, function the same. I didn't understand the language of the people around me. My language, my family, my life. All of it was gone.

"Charles was a chance at redemption. He worked so hard to free me. But it didn't matter. Nothing worked. I tried to teach him, tried to show him things about the time I lived in, thinking it might spark an idea. He could have used that information to change the face of what your people knew about Egypt at the time, but he knew no one would take him seriously. He couldn't just wake up one morning knowing everything he did about my dynasty, but still, he fought for me."

"How do you know he wasn't just using *you* for his own ends? Keeping you around as a novelty?"

He looked down and his shoulders drooped. "Honestly...I don't. Though I could read his mind as easily as I read yours and I found no such manipulation there. After he passed, I was heartbroken and lonely all over again.

"But then, a star to navigate by. I found out about you, heard Atef talk about a new Dr. Kent. So I did my own research. Yes, I made sure you got hired. I thought you'd be able to start where his journey had ended." He chuckled a little. "It was logical, yes? But perhaps it was a mistake."

It was logical. Given the circumstances, Elisa probably would have come to the exact same conclusion Nef had. Her anger deflated a little.

"I have looked, Nef."

"You didn't want to. And now, your search will end. Without my body here, I'll be too far away to remind you. Your life will progress. And mine, such as it is, will not."

Bastet purred against his feet again and tried to lick his leg. He bent down as if to touch her, and Elisa saw her fur rise like static was there.

"I hope you'll forgive me." He looked up from his knees at Elisa. "It seemed you wanted to be here and I needed you. The more I got to know you, the less important the search became. But Elisa, I can't go on like this," he looked down at his transparent form, "forever."

He stroked Bastet's head as she sat in front of him as if protecting him.

"You gifted yourself to me—your body and your mind—and I'm so grateful for that but it just reminds me of what I'm not. That I can't really have you or be with you. But I won't ask you to search any longer. I have to let you go. You must live the life you've been given. For me."

Elisa strode over to him. An errant lock of hair had fallen in his face. She reached her hand out to push it back and then stopped herself.

Instead, he took her hands in his and kissed her knuckles. "I have always believed that there's one soulmate for everyone. I've had the chance to know you, Elisa Kent. I can suffer through the rest of eternity without the feel of you on my lips and your touch on my hand or knowing how you smell, because I know the way your smile looks when you daydream, how your eyes sparkle in the Egyptian sun, and the things you think about when you think I'm not paying attention. That's better than any afterlife I could have imagined for myself."

He reached up slowly and touched her lips. She could actually feel it, so she knew it must have taken great effort. He flickered once or twice afterward but wouldn't admit how hard that one action had been.

"Will you stay with me tonight?"

"I would be honored."

"Nef…" There were no words. He was leaving. They would be alone again. At least now she had Bastet, but he would be truly alone in yet another new place that he hardly understood. She couldn't prevent this and she'd failed him. "I'm sorry."

"I know, ma cher. I am too."

Chapter Fifteen

When Elisa woke up the next morning, Nef was staring at her. His eyes crinkled and a smile started at the edges of his mouth.

"What are you smiling about?"

"You snore like a mouse."

"And how does a mouse snore?"

"Quietly. Peacefully."

Elisa chuckled. "At least it's not loud and obnoxious like your snoring."

"I don't snore."

"You most certainly do."

"Was I really snoring, or was I making you think I was snoring?"

Elisa pushed at his chest without thinking about it, but her hand didn't immediately go through him. There was a little bit of resistance, and she could almost feel the cotton of his shirt against her hand.

Her eyes flew up to his, but he seemed just as shocked as she was. "What the hell just happened?"

"I don't know. Do it again."

Elisa slowly reached out her hand and placed it against his chest. He wasn't quite solid, but he certainly was more than just a buzz.

His dark brown eyes opened wider at her touch. "I can feel you. Your hands are cold."

"How is this possible?" The longer her hand rested on his chest, the more solid he became.

"What do you feel?"

"I don't know. It's uncomfortable, but not painful."

"Can you describe it?"

He started to push her hand away but stopped. "I'm not research, Elisa. Just let me enjoy it."

He reached his hand up and threaded his fingers through her hair. Elisa inhaled at the feel of his skin against her scalp and closed her eyes. Before she could open them again, she felt Nef's lips crush against hers. His lips were soft against her own and he claimed them in a kiss that was neither soft nor romantic. It was desperate.

His hand traveled to the hem of her shirt to lift it and caress her stomach. His tongue tasted every bit of her mouth and explored every ridge while his hand worked its way even more slowly up her chest to her breast. They both groaned when he found her nipple and pinched just hard enough to send shivers down Elisa's body.

His mouth moved to her neck and he nipped at the skin just below her ear.

"I want to feel you."

Elisa tugged her shirt over her head and Nef sat up to do the same. When he shifted on the bed, it creaked a little under his now-weighted body.

He moved on top of Elisa to straddle her and she reached up to touch his chest and feel the warmth of his skin there.

Nef bent down to kiss her again and Elisa closed her eyes and raised her lips to meet him. But nothing happened.

When she opened her eyes, there was no one in the room but Bastet, licking her paw on the dresser across from the bed.

She knew it had been too good to be true. At first, Elisa had tried to convince herself that it had been some kind of weird lucid dream, but when she went to shower, she peeked in the mirror and the skin under her right ear was red where Nef had gently bitten her.

When she got out, she checked her work bag. His finger was missing. Now she was irritated *and* horny. How was this possible? What had even happened?

Atef was going to be pissed at her if she showed up to work and his new prized mummy had just disappeared overnight.

She finished getting ready and left for the lab as quickly as she could.

It was everything she could do to not run full speed through the museum and through the halls that led to her lab.

When she finally got through the door, Tomas was sitting in the chair in front of her computer, holding the heart scarab.

Elisa tried her best not to look as flustered as she felt.

"Morning, Tomas. Have you been here all night?"

Tomas turned the scarab over and over in his hands. He finally stopped and rubbed his thumb over the inscription.

"No, I got here early. I was going to finish packing the smaller items this morning, and I stumbled across this."

"Oh, interesting. Did you read it?"

"I did. I had to look at your transliteration to make much sense of it though. It's...kind of beautiful."

Elisa walked toward him and held out her hand.

"And very rare."

Tomas looked hesitant to hand it to her, but he eventually did.

"The strangest thing happened after I read it."

Elisa looked up at him. "Oh?"

"I'm not sure you'd believe me if I told you."

"Trust me. Some crazy things have happened in this lab." She leaned forward and whispered conspiratorially, "Atef thinks it's haunted." Elisa smiled at him as he shook his head.

"I might believe him."

"So what happened?"

"It seemed like, for just a moment, this shirtless man was standing behind me, and I felt a pop like the air had electricity in it, but then he just...vanished." Tomas shook his head. "You must think I'm crazy. I'm used to being outside. Maybe being closed up in here all day is making me antsy.

"Probably. Had any coffee this morning?"

Tomas scratched his stubble.

"Obviously not enough. I'm going to go grab a cup. Can I get you one?"

Elisa moved out of his way as he got up and started walking toward the door.

"That would be lovely, thanks. And, sorry about yesterday. I was in a bit of a mood."

"It's not a problem. There's a lot to do. One cream one sugar, right?"

"You have a good memory."

He still seemed a little confused about what had just happened, but he smiled and headed out the door.

As soon as the door closed, Elisa started whisper-shouting Nef's name. She didn't get any response.

She checked his mummy for the missing finger and was surprised to find that not only was it where it should have been, but it was reattached like it had never been removed to begin with.

She wanted to stop and write all of this down because there had to be a reason why that happened, but her most immediate concern was finding Nef. She called for him a few more times.

Suddenly, a notebook that had been sitting next to her computer collapsed to the floor. It had to be him, but why couldn't she see or hear him?

Her computer screen flashed on in front of her and she watched as the mouse moved to open a blank document. At least Nef still seemed to be able to move objects.

The keys clacked slowly, and she watched them depress into the keyboard in helplessness. What was he trying to tell her?

READSCARAB

Duh. Why hadn't she thought of that? Was it possible that when Tomas had read the scarab Nef had been transferred to him somehow? That meant that he could only be "visible" to one person at a time.

"Okay, hang on."

Elisa moved over to her magnifying lamp and flicked it on. It was hard to read in good light because the inscription was so worn. She read it out without stumbling over any of the words this time. As soon as she finished the last one, there was a *pop* like an outlet had blown and Nef was standing in front of her, looking much the same as he had in bed this morning, but much less visible and maybe a little scared.

"What the fuck?"

Now that Elisa's heart rate had slowed to its normal pace again, she could think about the events of the morning. The reason for Nef's disappearance was obvious, or seemed to be, but it didn't explain how he'd been made solid before he disappeared. His finger somehow reattaching itself also didn't make any sense.

"Tomas is going to be back any minute, but I need you to tell me what happened after he read the inscription."

Nef leaned against the counter where the computer sat.

"I don't really know. I was with you, and then I was here, watching Tomas. It felt like my body got sucked through a vacuum to get here. It was painful, but it was all just…black…for a few seconds before I was in here."

"Painful?"

He rubbed his goatee, "Yes, like a pins and needles feeling all over my body. But I felt so weak when I appeared here. I didn't make myself disappear, it just kind of happened on its own. That's usually something I control myself."

"Did you make yourself…solid, I guess, this morning?"

He looked at her and smiled sadly. "No. If I'd been able to do that, I would have done it long before now."

"So it seems like you're attached to whoever reads the scarab. My brain is spinning trying to figure all of this out. We could tell Thomas or Robert and see if you…transfer to them again."

He flickered again in front of her and a pained expression crossed his face. "No. Absolutely not. Some things are better left as mysteries, Elisa."

"But accurate replication is the basis for the scientific method."

Nef smiled gently at her. "No, love." He leaned over to her and touched his forehead to hers. "I'm just grateful I got to hold you at least once."

Elisa heard the keypad at the door beep. "Be in my head today, but go rest. You don't look like yourself."

Tomas entered, double-fisting two coffees, with Robert right behind him.

"Look who I found!"

"Seems like everyone is early today," Elisa said.

Tomas walked across the room and handed her a coffee. "Just the way you like it."

She heard Nef growl. *The last thing he knows is what you like. Please, can I hit him now?*

Elisa covered her chuckle with a small sip through the lid of her cup. *No. I think you startled him enough with the bag yesterday and then appearing today.*

Not well enough to make him leave, though.

More's the pity.

Elisa hadn't been paying attention to whatever question Robert had asked of her, so he asked again.

"Dr. Kent? Can we go ahead and start preparing the sarcophagus?"

She looked at him blankly.

"For transport?"

Will I still be able to see and talk to you for a while? She asked in her head.

Yes. I'll still be here.

"I don't see why not. Let's be very careful. We don't want anything falling off."

Nef chuckled in her ear.

She was going to miss that sound long after he was gone.

Chapter Sixteen

Elisa found an easy pace working with Thomas and Robert. Even if Thomas had been an asshole, his field experience balanced out nicely with Robert's lab experience and they shared stories as they worked. Elisa pretended to be listening and smiled here and there, but she was too lost to her own thoughts.

As she was placing soft cotton padding in the sides of the sarcophagus, she realized just how exhausted the last few days had left her. The emotional rollercoaster of being angry at Nef, finding she was in love with him, knowing he had to leave, and packing him off for the next ten years had not been easy to navigate. Her brain hurt and her emotions were so tangled up with one another that she barely even began to know where to untangle them. Focusing on work seemed like the solution so she didn't risk biting someone's head off.

Her life before Cairo had been boring by most people's standards, but lately, it had been anything but. She'd been a content workaholic before this endeavor.

She wouldn't fail Nef. Couldn't fail him. It might take her the whole ten years or longer to find that jar, but she would do it. She needed to be able to sit down and map out a plan of how to do that in more than a day, but if it took her the rest of her life, she would honor her promise to him. He deserved better than to be stuck between worlds. With a heaviness that made her hands shake, she realized she might be his last hope of ever entering the afterworld.

Go easy on yourself, ma cher. If anyone can do this, it's you. I'll find my peace.

Yeah, well, whatever happens to you once you get there is up to you.

She just hoped Osiris wouldn't judge him too harshly for the wrongs of someone centuries ago. Until recently, she'd have believed Osiris was just a God of myth, but Nef had changed so much of her perspective of what was myth, what was real, and where they blended together. What if all of the gods and goddesses that were just relics on walls and in museums were real?

She had a vague memory of her mother praying to Isis one night when she was very small. Maybe she'd light a candle and pray to Isis and Osiris tonight for good measure. What could it hurt?

Elisa moved to the back shelves to get more padding.

Nef?

I'm here.

I just wanted you to know that I'm going to do my best to find your heart.

I think you already have, he said.

I love you.

Until the serpent eats the sun, ma cher.

When they had done all they could do for the safety of Nef's remains to be transported, Elisa wandered up to Atef's office to let him know they were just waiting for the crew to arrive in the morning to load him into a crate.

"Excellent! You have exceeded my expectations, Dr. Kent."

"Thank you, Atef." Elisa turned to walk to her own office but stopped in the doorway.

"Can I ask you a strange question?"

"Certainly." He sat back in his chair.

"Why did you decide to hire me?"

"Ah," he leaned his elbows on the arms of his chair and steepled his fingers in front of his chest. "A number of reasons, actually. I remembered your parents from so long ago. Wonderful people. I also knew you were related to the infamous Dr. Kent who initially found this tomb and I thought it would be...what's the word? Ah, serendipitous of you to work on it. It seems I was correct in that regard. Ultimately, though, it was a board decision, and they were unanimous in it."

"But you did have other applicants?"

His brow furrowed slightly but then he smiled. "We thought we did. But when we looked at all of the resumes that were submitted, they were all yours. Of course, we could have promoted someone internally, but by fate or design, you were the right choice. It is as Allah wills it, Elisa."

She frowned at that. "You didn't think it was strange that all of the resumes were mine?"

"I thought it might just be a glitch in the software. But I didn't question it much. Some mysteries aren't meant to be solved." He opened his hands in a gesture of supplication. "Otherwise, they wouldn't be mysteries at all."

Elisa nodded. "Thank you, Atef. I'll start on the next lot tomorrow morning after they've cleared the lab tonight."

"I admire your work ethic, Elisa. But there's no real hurry to start on anything too soon. This was an exception, but I hope you'll soon see that the pace of life in Cairo is not like in America or London."

"I'll keep that in mind. Thanks, Atef."

Elisa walked into her office and mentally greeted the pyramids again.

I can never get over their beauty, Nef said from somewhere nearby. *They were imposing when I was a boy and that hasn't changed over the centuries.*

Are you here?

I'm behind you.

Elisa turned around and saw Nef adorned in the same way she'd seen him the first time they met. He had his linen kilt on and the collar, decked with precious stones. She hadn't noticed an image of the feather of the goddess Maat inlaid in the stones the first time, but as he was a vizir it fit his station. A *nemes* covered his head. He may have looked at home in modern clothing, but it was just an illusion. This is who he was born to be. What he was meant to stay.

"There are so many things I didn't get to ask you."

"I know. We have time. Write them down. I'll come back and hopefully, you'll still be here."

"I don't think I'll ever leave now."

"You'll have to get that bookshelf up and re-alphabetize your books."

Elisa smiled, but there was no joy in it. "I guess I'll have to."

"I...I want to ask something of you." He moved closer to her but seemed tentative.

"Anything."

"Destroy the scarab."

Elisa was mortified. "Nef, I can't. First of all, it's packed away with you. Secondly, no. What if I need it to...awaken you again or something when you get back."

"It's not packed away anymore. You'll find it where you least expect it, but I don't want to run the risk of someone else reading it and taking me away from my attachment to you. The distance will likely be too great for me to communicate with you, but I want to know we still have some sort of connection while I'm gone."

"If you've hidden it from me, I can't destroy it."

"Then keep it safe until I come back to you."

"I'll be old and haggard by then. Are you sure you don't want some other beautiful woman to stumble upon it?" She trailed a finger over her desk, not capable of looking at him when he answered.

Nef walked over to her and placed his forehead against hers in a gesture she'd come to realize was more intimate to him than even a kiss. "Never, my love."

Elisa let a tear escape while the hum resonated against her skin. She hated saying goodbye.

"I'm going to be so lonely without you."

"And I without you. If I could do one more thing in my time in Cairo, it would be to visit the Nile and put a new lotus in the river when the moon is high. For the next four centuries, I'd wish for you."

"I'd wish for you, too."

She felt the vibration of him trail his fingers over her lips and into her hair.

"You should go home and rest. Tomorrow will be busy and you look exhausted."

"I don't want to leave you. I could sleep on the sofa here."

Nef smiled and rubbed his thumb against her cheek. "I don't want to leave you either. But I think it's best this way. Go be in your own bed and let Bastet comfort you. She is the goddess of protection, after all. I know she'll keep you safe for me."

"Will I see you in the morning?"

"Would you like to?"

"What kind of question is that?"

"I don't want you to hurt any more than you already do. I can hear your loud thoughts, but your pain is louder. I can feel it echoing my own." She looked up into his eyes. He was so close and seemed so real. She saw the hurt in his eyes that felt like it mirrored her own.

"Watching them put you on the truck will be hard, but if I have to watch that, then yes, I'd like to see you one last time."

"Then you shall. Sleep well, ma cher. Say an extra prayer to the God of All for me tonight, too, for I fear he stopped listening to me long ago."

Nef kissed the top of her head and then her lips. She reveled in the vibration of him against her skin. And then he was gone.

Elisa didn't even have the energy to even cry when she finally got home. Her body felt too heavy to carry her, so she collapsed on the couch. All she could think about was Nef. They'd only been apart for an hour or so, and she knew the longing was only going to get worse as the days passed. She needed a distraction.

Searching for the jar would have been a good one, but it required more mental energy than she was willing to expend right now. She realized she hadn't checked her personal email since before she left for the dig. Aunt Mae probably thought she'd died.

Elisa hefted her tablet out of her bag and saw that she had over two-hundred unread emails. Most of them were junk, but at least fifty of them were from Aunt Mae. She wasn't about to respond to all of them, but she read them in order from oldest to newest. Most of them detailed Mae's various illnesses, real and imagined. The more recent ones got more urgent; Mae knew she was busy but did she not have time for her crazy aunt at all and so on.

Elisa typed a quick reply.

    Hi Mae. Lots going on. Thank you for sending the journals with Miriam. Make her take you to dinner when she comes home. Can we catch up on a video call soon? Let me know when you're free.
    Love,
    E

Elisa sighed and put the tablet on the coffee table. Bastet jumped up onto her stomach and began to purr as soon as Elisa touched her head.

"You're not leaving, right?"

Bastet licked her chin in response.

"Good. I can't have everyone I love leave me."

Elisa remembered her earlier thought about praying to Isis and Osiris. She picked up Bastet and placed her under her arm while she went to hunt down a candle. The boxes in the library were the most likely place. Bastet jumped out of her arms and ran ahead of her, but when Elisa went into the room, the little cat was nowhere to be seen.

"Where did you go, little mother?"

A soft meow came from one of the boxes in the far corner of the room. Elisa managed a smile as she crossed over to it and lifted the flap to reveal two big, glossy yellow eyes staring back at her.

"Are we playing hide and seek? Because if we are, I think you lost."

Bastet pushed her head into Elisa's head and purred then jumped out of the box. She rubbed against the corner of it and sat looking up at Elisa expectantly.

"All right, I guess I'll look in it."

When she lifted the flaps again, Elisa was surprised to find incense cones and candles packed away with some other small artifacts she'd kept over the years. There was an Eye of Horus incense burner along with a hieroglyphic of Isis and Osiris printed on old papyrus. It had been her mother's. The goddess and god had been hand-painted in their royal finery and stood close together standing over cartouches of their names printed beneath them.

She wasn't much of one for candles and scents, but as she lifted the incense to her nose and inhaled, she had a memory of her mother enjoying the scents of sandalwood and myrrh and burning them every full moon when she'd been little.

She knelt down and retrieved a few of the white pillar candles, the incense holder, a cone of incense, and even a lighter that had been tossed carelessly in the bottom of the box. On instinct, she lifted the image of the gods out, too.

There wasn't much room in the library, so she took her items out to the coffee table in the living room. She set the three pillar candles up in a triangle on the table with the incense in the middle of them and the image of Isis and Osiris under that. Bastet jumped on the table and headbutted a pillar candle as Elisa lit the incense.

"Fire isn't for cats." Bastet continued to rub on the center candle as Elisa lit the other two. Bastet finally jumped over on the sofa with Elisa as she lit the wick on the last candle.

"I don't know what to do, really. The moon isn't full either. Think it matters?" Bastet jumped into her lap, kneading her legs, and Elisa resigned herself to just talking to the image.

"Mother Isis, Father Osiris, I don't know if I'm doing this right, but I wanted to ask you...to protect him. Keep him safe. Help us find the answers so he can be set free."

The incense whirled around her, and Elisa was suddenly so drowsy she wasn't sure that she'd be able to keep her eyes open. The warmth of Bastet on her lap brought her comfort and she suddenly felt that everything would be okay.

Bastet licked her paw and then watched the smoke from the incense cloud around them. It wasn't long before Elisa was sound asleep under her.

Some part of her knew she must be dreaming. She was in Nef's version of Egypt. She was wearing a fine linen tunic that barely grazed the tops of her bare feet. She felt the cloth of it like a gentle kiss all over her body. The scent of sandalwood surrounded her and she glanced at her hands, surprised to find a heavy clay lotus in them with a lit candle nestled in the center. She was standing at the top of a massive stone staircase with fires blazing in braziers all around her. She felt pulled to follow the stairs down, the stone warm under her feet as if it had just been warmed by the sun.

The stars shone brightly overhead. She was so mesmerized by the clarity of them that she could have stood there for hours, just counting them. But something tugged at her to continue. It seemed to take hours to get to the bottom of the massive stone steps, but at the base of them was a sandy bank, and just a few feet from that was the dark water of the Nile.

She crossed the heated bank of the sand, feeling each grain between her toes. No thoughts were racing in her mind tonight. Just the peace of knowing what she was supposed to do. Without a pause, she crossed into the waters of the Nile. The warmth of it surrounded her until she was up to her waist in this living presence. The sound of her own voice startled her as she uttered words that were foreign to her, but somehow felt right. She bent to gently place the clay lotus in the rushing water and wished aloud for Nef to find his heart and find peace. Reluctantly, she withdrew her hands from the clay and watched as the lotus and the candle bobbed on the surface of the water. As it floated, Elisa watched as it made its way to the horizon and eventually to the stars where the light of the candle seemed to take its place amongst the other wishes in the firmament above.

Chapter Seventeen

One week later

She hadn't had time to say goodbye to Nef in a way that satisfied her. The loading of the truck started early on Thursday morning, and she had too much to oversee before the flight left for New York to spend any time alone with him. He'd stayed with her in her mind until the very last minute, and it felt as though she'd shipped her own heart off with him.

Miriam had been right though. Solving the puzzle, ignoring the people had worked for her so far and she didn't see any reason why she couldn't continue that thinking. As soon as she'd gotten back into the lab, she'd started making a spreadsheet of the most likely places to look for the jar. She'd already checked the most obvious, but it was worth looking into the broken jars that were already on the GEM's campus, just to be sure. She itemized the lot numbers and would systematically look at each one of them and then rule them out. She was already starting at a net negative because there were at least fifty to look at on the premises.

Atef had reminded her she had time in Cairo, but at this point, it looked like this would be a search that would take her a lifetime.

It would have been helpful to pull what she was coming to think of as her team together to help her search, but that would mean explaining everything to them. Tomas might have believed her, but he might also decide to have her committed, or worse: fired.

Instead, she set Tomas and Robert to the task of transferring the next items that would need to be cataloged, photographed, and x-rayed. Another mummy needed identifying and she couldn't ignore all of the work that Atef had hired her for in favor of her side project.

She decided after the first day of searching that she'd dedicate her weekends to it, but also wanted to get some time for getting out and exploring the city she'd barely had time to see.

In a month, she'd be giving a lecture as part of the spring lectureship series at the GEM but that speech could practically write itself. She wished Paoula would call and say she needed her in the field again, but the season was wrapping up and she didn't think that distraction was likely.

Elisa sat back in her work chair while Tomas and Robert listened to jazz and worked carefully on a collection that had been recovered from hidden Nazi archives in the late 1940s. It had been hiding in the basement of the British Museum since then, but a few years ago, the Egyptian government had negotiated its repatriation back to Cairo. There hadn't been space for it before the GEM had opened, but now that there was, it was time to get to work uncovering these new treasures.

They were from the end of the New Kingdom when Alexander the Great had moved in, and that was Tomas' specialty. She was happy to have him lead the way on this particular project. He lit up like a happy Golden Retriever puppy anytime they opened a new cardboard box, and it almost made her smile and the ache subside. Almost.

She had never been one to bring her personal life to work. Not that she'd had much of a personal life to discuss anyway, but Atef, Tomas, and Robert had started to notice her daily melancholy. Tomas took it upon himself to try to cheer her up with coffee and relics, while Atef left little gifts on her desk of fruit or native flowers and had asked her more than once to join him and his family for dinner or a trip to the market.

She had declined all of those invitations so far, but she wouldn't be able to keep that up forever. She'd been trying to work on her brave face, but it slipped every now and again, and one of the three of them would catch her staring off into space.

"What's that?" Tomas asked Robert as he opened another box and pulled out an ancient-looking piece of papyrus.

Elisa was staring mindlessly at the photographs they'd just taken that morning of the smaller parts of this collection.

"I don't know. It doesn't look like it belongs with this though. It looks...much older."

Tomas reached out with his gloved hands to retrieve the object in question.

Elisa glanced at him and saw that the papyrus was tied with a scrap of dyed-red linen. It was frayed along the edges. It looked like a million other scrolls she'd seen over the years. More often than not, they turned out to be accounting ledgers or even grocery lists of the ancients.

"Huh," remarked Tomas. "This looks like hieratic. Definitely not from this collection. Dr. Kent might want to have a look at this one."

She ignored him.

He held it up to the light. "Look there, it looks like something has been written over the original inscription." He squinted at the ancient ink and papyrus over his head.

"Is that...I can't make it out. Nef..."

Elisa whipped her head around and was out of her chair before he said another word. She almost reached for the papyrus but then remembered she didn't have gloves on.

She ran over to the cabinet. *Calm down, woman. Nef is a common prefix in ancient Egyptian. It could be a reference to Nefertiti for all you know.*

The cabinet door slammed behind her as she pulled the gloves over her sweaty hands.

"Let me see, Tomas." She practically snatched the scroll right out of his hands.

"The woes of Neferamun," She read aloud.

"Who's that?" Robert asked.

Elisa didn't even hear his question. "I can't read the rest of it. It's obscured by the rest of the text that's been written over it. Grab the portable x-ray and the UV. Let's see if we can see what's underneath the new text."

Her heart pounded in her ears. She hadn't thought much about the scroll that Nef had mentioned lately, but this could be a much-needed piece of the puzzle. She set the papyrus gently on the table and practically jumped up and down next to Tomas.

"Tomas, I could kiss you!"

He blushed a little. "Thank you, but who is Neferamun?"

She had to lie.

"I don't know. But isn't it wonderful that we don't? A new mystery ready to reveal itself."

Two hours later, Elisa had clear images of the original writing and a fully translated scroll of what she thought was the story of how Nef had been prevented from entering the afterlife. The scroll also included what could be the spell to set him free. It had been written by another priest who was probably a contemporary of Nef's and who seemed to take pity on him for what had happened to him.

According to the scroll, Neferaue had seen how close Nef was getting with Tuthmos and the influence he was beginning to have again as a statesman, politician, and noble. Nef wanted peace in the Kingdom, but Neferaue was only interested in becoming pharaoh herself as her mother had been before her. To do that, she needed the kingdom at odds so she could take the throne. She first plotted to make Nef fall in love with her and secret her away. When that failed to turn her half-brother against Nef, she took matters into her own hands and poisoned him, making it look like an assassination attempt.

The last line before the spell at the end read: "I alone know the truth. This is why my brother was felled."

She'd read that line over and over again until it was seared into her neurons. This priest must have known that he was powerless to help Nef in life but did what he could. She didn't know if this priest had tried to set Nef free into the afterlife himself or if he hoped that someone else would try. Either way, she was grateful for him.

A notification on her phone chimed and reminded her that she had her video call with Aunt Mae in an hour.

"Bollocks," she muttered to herself as she put her phone back in her pocket.

"Problem?" Tomas asked.

"Not really. I just have a date with my eccentric aunt soon."

"Mae? Is she still alive?"

Elisa chuckled. "And kicking. You remember her?"

"Of course. She intimidated the hell out of me."

Robert had left for the day and only she and Tomas were left in the lab, the rest of the museum quiet.

"Find anything interesting in that scroll? You've been working on it for a while."

"Maybe." She couldn't tell him she'd solved a part of one of the biggest puzzles that had ever landed in her lap. "It's hard to tell just yet."

"I've been meaning to ask you about that picture you have taped up on the cabinet there." Tomas nodded to the old photograph of Charles Kent inside Nef's tomb. "That's your great-grandfather and the tomb we just sent off to New York, right?"

Elisa glanced up at it too. "It is. He was one of the first ones in it."

"It's pretty amazing that you both got to work on it. I can't imagine that happens very often." Tomas stood up and walked over to look at it again. "What a legacy. You look a little like him."

"Do I?"

"Well, apart from the hat, glasses, and suit. Your faces are shaped similarly. Same nose. Same shape to the lips."

He leaned in to look a little more closely. "Are there five jars in this photo?"

"There are."

"But I only remember packing four."

"It went missing somewhere along the line. I've been looking for it, but I'm not sure we'll ever find it. It would have been nice to include it in the rest of the collection."

"It certainly is unique. Is that Hathor on the top?"

"As far as I can tell."

"Wonder why they needed a fifth one."

"That's a story for another day." Elisa stood up and slung her workbag over her shoulder, switched off her computer.

"Well, you're good at what you do. Maybe you'll find it where you least expect it."

She half-smiled and shrugged at him. "Maybe someday." Elisa took one last look at the picture and started toward the door. She turned around halfway across the lab.

"Thank you, Tomas. For all of your help. I just...wanted you to know I appreciate it."

Tomas nodded. "You're welcome. G'night, Elisa."

"Night, Tomas."

Elisa felt hopeful for the first time since before she'd heard Nef was leaving. The jar still seemed a long way off, but today's discovery went a long way toward lifting her spirits.

Even gearing herself up for listening to her aunt complain about her long list of ailments wasn't going to dismay her. She unlocked her tablet and clicked on the app to speak to her aunt two minutes early. Aunt Mae was already waiting.

Her grey hair was up in its usual bun, with unruly pieces sticking out on the sides. The screen of her aunt's laptop was tilted too far up, so Elisa could only see her forehead and glasses. Elisa's face reflected back to her in the lenses. She tried not to laugh, but did manage to get out an excited, "Hi, Auntie."

Mae's mouth moved but there was no sound. "You're muted, Mae. Click the little microphone in the bottom left corner."

There was a few moments' pause and then she heard her. "Did I do it? Can you hear me?"

"Yes. Well done. Now tilt your screen down so I can see your beautiful face."

Mae reached up and adjusted the screen. "Better?"

"Yes. Lovely."

Mae adjusted herself on screen and then finally seemed to remember her niece was also on. "Darling, you look lovely. Look at that smile! Is work going well, then?"

Elisa rested her elbow on the back of the couch and then placed her head against her knuckles. "Yeah. I had a bit of a time of it last week, but we made a good find today, so that's very exciting."

"Well done, you. I knew America wasn't where you needed to be. Egypt is where the fun is had."

Bastet had been mostly absent since Elisa got home, but she jumped on her stomach and sniffed the tablet.

"Who's that, darling? Do you have a cat? She's beautiful."

Elisa laughed as Bastet tried to lick the screen.

"I do. Her name is Bastet. She kind of adopted me, I think."

"What an excellent name. Bastet was always my favorite goddess. Oh, hold on. Your cousin wants to say hello."

Mae moved over slightly to allow Theo to bend down and share the screen with her. He pushed the laptop back to get both of them in frame and Elisa realized they were in her grandfather's study.

"Hiya, cos," he waved at her. Bastet had settled down and was purring on her again.

"Hello, good sir. How are you?"

"Good. Did you hear Miriam is back in town?"

"She came to see me before she left and she told me. I guess you're off of plant duty now."

He laughed. She'd never realized how much *he* looked like their great-grandfather until now. Even down to the glasses. If Tomas hadn't pointed out her likeness to him, she may never have noticed.

"Until she's off again at any rate."

"That's enough," said Mae, pushing him off. "This is my time with Elisa. You can schedule your own video call with her if you want." He waved and blew a kiss at her as he left the screen.

"Okay. Now I want to hear everything. Start at the beginning. What's your apartment like? How's Cairo? What are you working on?" A shrill alarm blasted through Elisa's speakers.

"What is that?"

"Blasted thing." Her aunt pressed the off switch. "Hang on, darling. I have to go take my meds. Two shakes. Don't go anywhere."

Elisa smiled at her aunt and scratched Bastet between the ears. She glanced briefly at the screen and remembered how much she'd loved that room when she was a teenager. It was filled to the brim with knickknacks, books, tools, busts, and any and everything that the scientists before her could fill it with. It was a maximalist's dream.

The sun was just beginning to set in London, and she could see it streaming through the window. There was a tall bookshelf placed behind the desk where her aunt sat, and she studied the objects there while she waited.

She glanced back down at Bastet, but then sharply raised her head again to look at the top of the bookshelf. Sitting toward the back, behind a gold astrolabe was what appeared to be a canopic jar. With the horns of a cow and the face of a woman.

"Hathor..."

Chapter Eighteen

"Mae! Mae!" There was no way Elisa was seeing what she thought she was seeing.

Mae showed back up on the screen a moment later. "What is it, Elisa?"

"Behind you on the filing cabinet. What is that?"

Mae looked behind her. "The astrolabe?"

Elisa tried not to roll her eyes. "No, behind that. The jar."

Mae walked over to the jar and picked it up. She brought it carefully over to the screen to show Elisa.

"This?"

Elisa's jaw dropped. It had been in her great-grandfather's study this whole time. There was no mistaking the intricately carved head of Hathor. Mae turned the jar over in her hands.

"Be careful with it. Don't open it!"

Mae seemed perplexed. "What is it, darling?"

"Something I've been looking for."

Mae placed it carefully on the desk like a bomb she was afraid would detonate.

"Why would he keep it?" Elisa asked more to herself than her aunt.

"Dr. Kent had a penchant for keeping all kinds of memorabilia from his digs."

Elisa was simultaneously pleased and horrified. It's possible her great-grandfather was worried that this piece of history would fall into the wrong hands, but with everything he knew about Nef, surely there's no way he ignored the possibility that this very jar contained the heart that Nef had been looking for for so long.

"He wrote about so much in his journals, but not about this. I wonder why."

"He was an enigma for sure. And a little eccentric. It runs in the family, I suppose." Mae tried a smile, but seeing Elisa's face, just shrugged. "What do you want me to do with it, love?"

"Nothing. I'm coming home to get it. Just leave it there and for the love of all that's holy, don't move it or open it."

"Can you afford to come home? I mean, you just started this job."

"The tomb that belongs with, I just sent the rest of the collection to New York. I'm pretty sure my boss will let me come retrieve it and see that it gets to the rest of the collection where it belongs."

"Very well, darling." Mae smoothed out the papers on her desk. "Now, tell me what you've been up to."

Elisa wanted to do anything but that. All she could think about was getting to London and getting back to Nef. She had the scroll, and she might have his heart right in front of her. She could fulfill her promise to him and set him free. Her heart squeezed at the prospect of what that meant, but she couldn't think about herself. Nef wouldn't be miserable for the rest of forever. He could be free to dwell in the afterlife with the people he loved. The people who understood him.

What a gift that must be, Elisa thought as she tried to engage in a somewhat meaningful conversation with her aunt. She wanted to call Atef now, get him to buy her a ticket, and just go home, but even she had to admit that it would be hard to convince Atef of any real urgency. After four-thousand years, what was a few more days?

She drifted in and out of the two-hour conversation with Mae, which mostly consisted of filling Elisa in on gossip about people she didn't know and the list of Mae's real and imagined diagnoses, which had apparently gotten much longer in the last few months.

Eventually, Mae yawned for the third time in one sentence and Elisa interrupted.

"I think I should let you get some sleep, Aunt."

Mae smiled as she wiped at her tired, grey eyes. "Oh, but I do so love being able to catch up with you."

Elisa smiled and her heart warmed. In the midst of Nef and grieving her parents every day, she often forgot that she still had people in her life who loved and valued her.

"I do too. I'll be home soon, though. And we can schedule more video dates."

"A capital idea, darling. I miss you and love you more than words can say. I hope you know that, always."

"I do. I love you, too."

"If you really loved me, you'd give me some babies to snuggle."

Elisa wasn't even a little bit insulted, but she still pretended to be. "Aunt! There's plenty of time for that. But maybe one day."

"Hopefully that day comes before I'm in my grave."

"Goodnight, Aunt Mae. Kisses."

Elisa rolled her eyes and chuckled before she closed her laptop.

Bastet took the opportunity to jump on her lap and headbutt her.

"I haven't forgotten about you, little mother. Would you like to eat?"

Instead of jumping off down and padding to the kitchen, Bastet started kneading Elisa in the abdomen then turned in a circle twice and laid on her.

"I guess I live here now since you won't let me up and I'm certainly not about to move you."

Elisa scratched her between the ears and she felt the purr reverberate through her body.

"Tomorrow is going to be a big day, I think. I hope Atef is agreeable to me leaving again so soon. Don't worry. I'll only be gone a few days. I'll leave the window open for you, and lots of food. It's just for work anyway. Surely Atef will see how incredible it would be for there to be five canopic jars on display."

Bastet lifted her head and blinked judgmental green eyes at Elisa as if to say she didn't believe it was about work in the slightest.

Elisa watched the lights of London come into view from the plane window. She had a love/hate relationship with being here. It wasn't that it reminded her of her parents because they had hardly spent much time together here; it was the memory of the grieving she'd gone through afterward. Sometimes the loss of them still made her chest ache with a love that had no place to go. She imagined that must be how Nef felt, too.

But there were happy memories here. Memories with Theo and her aunt, both of whom had pulled her out of that grief. Or at least offered her a lifeboat amid the waves.

It just hadn't felt like home. Nowhere had, really.

Nef feels like home. She wasn't even conscious of having the thought, but it was there. Nef had understood her. Partly because he could hear her thoughts, and honestly, maybe that's what she'd needed all along since she often didn't have the words to tell people what she needed or how she was feeling. Emotions were complicated, illogical things.

She'd have to be brave. Everyone left in one way or another. She'd thought that people just left her, but she should know better than most that death was objective. Days ended. Years ended. Centuries ended. Civilizations collapsed and were rebuilt.

It was the rebuilding of her own life that she'd be focused on now. She'd have to go on without Nef's presence in her life if she did manage to somehow break this spell. She couldn't wait to see him, but she was terrified that seeing him again meant truly letting him go this time.

Atef would keep her busy. He'd been thrilled when she told him about the fifth jar. Less thrilled that it had been hidden away in a dusty study for who-knew-how-many years, but the fact that there was no other fifth canopic jar in recorded history soothed his feathers and his ego. This find would always be attached to the GEM.

When she finally disembarked from the plane and wandered to the exit, she wasn't surprised to find that her Aunt Mae had hired a car for her. The driver greeted her warmly and confirmed the location of her aunt's house.

The ride took less than ten minutes without traffic and Elisa was at least somewhat happy to see the old, red brickwork as they pulled up to the house.

Before she could get out of the car, the front door was opening, and Mae, Theo, and Miriam were scurrying out of the house like mice called by the Pied Piper.

Theo was the first to greet her. She'd never loved hugs, but Theo's were always warm and healing. And for some reason, he always smelled like patchouli. Elisa let herself lean into him, realizing that she'd gone far too long without any real human touch.

"Hey stranger," he said into her ear. "I've missed you, too."

He pulled away before Mae knocked them both over. She opened her arms in invitation and Elisa went into them willingly.

"Hi Aunt. It's so good to see you."

"We're happy to have you home, darling. Even if it's too brief."

"My turn!" Miriam chimed in from the sidelines.

"You've just seen her, haven't you?" Theo chided.

"Well, yes, but she is *my* best friend." Elisa leaned into Miram's side hug and smiled at their constant bickering.

"You may be the best friend, but I might as well be her brother."

"Does that make you better than me?"

Elisa chimed in, "Now, now, children. There's no need to fight over me. I love you both equally."

Mae grabbed Elisa's hand and led her to the house while Theo tipped the driver and grabbed Elisa's bag.

"I've had dinner prepared for you. I know you just told me about all of your adventures, but I'd love to hear more about the dig."

"It wasn't really all that exciting."

Mae ushered them into the dark dining room, lit with candles. Elisa felt like she'd stepped back in time or onto a gothic movie set. It always took her a moment to readjust to Mae's flair for the dramatic, even in her style of decorating and mood-setting.

"It's Egypt, darling. It's always exciting," Mae looked wistful as she sat down, smoothed her napkin on her lap, and served herself peas.

"I did identify a mummy that Tomas had spent months on. It was actually—"

"Wait," Theo stopped her. "Why does that name sound familiar?"

"Because he dumped her in college."

Theo almost choked on his wine. "*That* Tomas? What was he doing within a hundred yards of you?"

"He was working at the dig site. Still doing the job he dumped me for. But he's actually working at the GEM now...as my assistant."

Theo cackled. "That bastard. I hope you give him hell every day."

"Oh, Theo," Miriam ran her finger along the edge of her glass, "I would do that. But not our Elisa. She's too kind."

Elisa looked at her pointedly. "You almost make that sound like an insult."

Miriam smiled at her. "It's not. You are kind. You see people as you want them to be, not as they are. That's a gift and a curse, I suppose. But he doesn't matter anyway. Elisa has a new male friend. Are you going to see him when you go to New York?"

This time, Elisa gave her a look that was far more scathing. Miriam just raised her eyebrows like she hadn't just opened the floodgates.

Mae twittered, the gossip of Tomas totally forgotten. "A new man you say? You must tell us all about him."

Elisa stayed silent.

"Well, from what I hear, he's in antiques and he just got transferred to New York. Are you going to see him while you're there?"

Elisa tried to kick Miriam under the table but just ended up whacking her shin on the table leg instead. She coughed to cover her pain and the discomfort she felt at her family knowing anything about Nef. Even if most of it was a lie.

"That's wonderful news, darling. Are you going to be able to see him?"

Elisa lifted her own wine glass, looking deeply at the amber liquid. "I hope so. We left with the understanding that we probably wouldn't be seeing each other for some time. He's probably forgotten about me by now."

"You seem wistful when you talk about him. You must love him."

"Professor, you are far too observant for your own good."

"I may have been a widow for the last sixty years," Mae began, "but there's one thing I know, 'I hold it true, whate'er befall; I feel it when I sorrow most. 'Tis better to have love and lost than never to have loved at all.' Tennyson said that, you know?"

"Cheer up, Els." Theo raised his glass to her. "I'm sure he hasn't. You'd be a hard one to forget." He tilted his glass at Miriam. "And that one even harder, as she's so pigheaded and stubborn."

A roll went flying and hit Theo square in the forehead.

"That was a compliment!"

"Be that as it may," Elisa said stiffly. "I think this will truly be the last time I see him."

Miriam reached across the table and grabbed and patted Elisa's hand. "Don't dwell there, *cher*. It's a bad place to stay. What if we have a girl's night? Do our hair, paint our nails, watch bad movies til the sun comes up."

"Thanks, Mir. I'd love to, but I have to be up early tomorrow to be at the museum."

"Ah, yes. There's our girl. Work work work and no play." Theo scolded.

This time, Elisa grabbed a roll and chucked it at Theo, but it missed his head by a foot. Miriam snickered and Elisa erupted in laughter too. It felt good to be home.

Even through her gloves, Elisa felt the grooves of the clay. If she closed her eyes, she could almost see one of Nef's images in her imagination of the priest who would have held this jar long before she did. Did he know Nef? Did he love him and mourn his death? Did he fear him?

Hathor's mighty face stared up at her and almost dared her to open it, but she knew she couldn't. After so many centuries, if there was anything in this jar, it could crumble to dust just by being exposed to oxygen. No, the safer bet was to wait. But her own heart pounded in her ears at the idea that she might be holding Nef's in her hands now.

The light in the study was dim. She'd snuck in here after dinner when the rest of her family had gone up to bed, not willing to wait a moment longer to finally see the jar.

She turned it over carefully in the light of the desk lamp.

Her heart stopped.

In the back of the jar, just below Hathor's head, was a crack. It ran from the seal to the base. It was impossible to know if it ran all the way through the clay and if anything inside might have been damaged.

Maybe this was why her grandfather had kept it. Even he would have known that any tissue inside would be obliterated if exposed to air for too long. Did he keep it from Nef, knowing there would be no hope of sending him back to the afterworld he so longed for? Or had he decided to keep it even before he'd met Nef?

"What was going on in your mind, old man?"

She knew she would never get an answer to that question. If it wasn't in Charles' journals, it wouldn't be anywhere.

Elisa took out her recorder. Just because she wasn't in her lab, didn't mean she would slip on following the process.

"Canopic jar with the head of Hathor. Appears to be the same as in the photograph of Ne–" she stopped herself, then cleared her throat, "the tomb. Similar appearance and coloration as the other four jars, although this one appears lighter as though exposed to sunlight."

She turned the jar again, slowly. "Markings on the bottom of the jar indicate that once again, the name of the deceased has been scored off with some type of tool. Jar is approximately..." she pulled out her measuring tape, "twenty-five centimeters in height, including the head, which is congruent to the other four jars in the collection.

"Unfortunately, the jar has incurred a crack to the posterior side, of unknown origin. X-Ray and/or MRI will be able to discern if the contents, if any, have been damaged or altered. Otherwise, the jar is in exceptional condition."

"Working theory is that the heart of our unknown mummy could be located inside. If so, this would be the first of its kind on record."

Knowing Atef would want to see this fabled fifth jar, she took out her phone and snapped a few pictures to send to Atef. It was late to be sending them, although she admitted she didn't know much about Atef's sleeping habits. She sent them anyway, hoping he'd be surprised when he woke up.

A few minutes later, her phone alerted her to a new message:

AMAZING! I wish I could see it in person. I've emailed the British Museum and let them know to expect you. New York has also heard the news and knows you'll be coming soon.

"And he calls me a workaholic," she said to the empty space. She half-expected a smart-ass response from Nef, but there was nothing.

She packed the jar in a small crate she'd brought with her, lined in soft foam. Hathor stared up at her, her features clear and meticulously crafted.

"I hope you've kept his heart safe for me after all this time."

Elisa closed and latched the lid on the wooden crate and carried it up to her room with her.

As she changed for bed, she knew sleep would probably elude her. She didn't have Bastet to purr on her and soothe her. And while she was overjoyed to have found the jar, it could turn out to be another dead end for Nef. Either way, she'd have to take the jar to New York but what would she tell him if his heart had disintegrated?

She ran through a thousand conversations with him in her mind, and before she knew it, the sun was rising and she felt worse than she did the night before.

Her hands shook as she buttoned her white shirt and put on her khaki slacks. She couldn't remember the last time she'd been this nervous. It was her job to solve the problems, but right now, there was nothing she could do. Being out of control and not knowing the answer was foreign to her. Facts were comfortable and logical, and she felt ungrounded not knowing if this jar find was going to break Nef more than he'd already been broken.

Chapter Nineteen

The British Museum felt dark and stuffy in comparison to the very modern GEM. She was greeted at the entrance by Dr. Nicole Worthy, the new curator. Elisa felt frumpy in her standard outfit next to the elegant woman walking toward her who could have been a Nordic model. The smile she gave her was genuine, though.

"Dr. Kent, a pleasure. It's an honor to meet the granddaughter of the famous Dr. Charles Kent, as well."

Elisa's neck felt hot. "Oh, well...thank you."

"I'm a bit of a fan, myself. I think I've read just about everything you've ever published. And my colleagues at Jaen were tickled pink when you identified that mummy so quickly a few weeks ago."

Now, Elisa's palms were sweaty.

"It was really nothing."

"Nothing?" Dr. Worthy stopped mid-stride to turn to Elisa. "Don't sell yourself short, my friend. There are far too few magnificent women in this field as it is. Self-deprecation doesn't suit you. Best to learn to say 'thank you,' and take the praise that's given."

Elisa knew that if she'd held a mirror up to her face in that moment her cheeks would be flaming red. She wanted to argue, but instead, she took a deep breath and simply said, "Thank you."

"Much better. Now, I've got everything set up. Dr. Tawfik sent me the photographs you took. We don't have quite the set up that you do back home, but hopefully, it'll do."

Dr. Worthy opened a secure door and Elisa saw an excited team standing in wait behind it. They all introduced themselves and Elisa forgot their names the second they said them. She would have written them in her notebook, but the crate occupied both of her hands.

One of the taller gentlemen on the team looked at her expectantly, and she reluctantly handed over the crate.

"Not to worry," Dr. Worthy said. "It's in good hands. We'll get you copies of everything to send back to the GEM. You're welcome to wait in my office if you'd like."

"I'd actually rather stay here if that's all right."

Dr. Worthy smiled. "Ah, I'd expected as much. A woman after my own heart who wants to make sure everything is done properly. We'll start with the x-ray, shall we, Tim?"

The tall man who'd taken the crate wandered off into a side room with an x-ray machine. There was a glass partition, so Elisa could watch him set everything up. It seemed to take forever, but she was glad he was being careful with the crate and its contents.

Finally, it was ready. The radiographer sat behind a desk with a large monitor and told Elisa that the picture should be up within a minute or two.

Sweat began to form on Elisa's temples and nape as she stared at the screen, willing Nef's heart to be intact.

Prayers may have been foreign to her, but she tried again, *Isis, Osiris, if you ever held any love for Nef or me, please let his heart be here.*

"Image coming in,"

The picture was slow to load, but the image soon began to form Hathor's head in black and white, followed by grainy shadows and light.

"It'll just take a moment to clear," the radiographer said.

Elisa's heart was pounding so loudly, she was sure everyone in the room could hear it.

Then, the image appeared. Nestled in the bottom of the jar was clearly muscular tissue. It had been wrapped in linen, but the definition was still there.

"Oh my god," Dr. Worthy whispered reverently beside her.

"Is that...?" One of the team asked.

"A human heart," Elisa answered. "The only one ever known to exist inside of a canopic jar."

The room was silent.

"Remarkable, Dr. Kent."

"This is a once-in-a-lifetime find, Dr. Kent," said the radiographer, "honored to be in the room with you."

Other murmurs of congratulations went up around the room with random pats on Elisa's back that she tried to shrug off. She was about to say something to deflect, but she glanced at Dr. Worthy, and simply said "thank you."

Dr. Worthy tilted her head over to the far side of the room for Elisa to join her there.

"Listen, I don't usually do this, but…well, you're about to be the most famed Egyptologist of this century."

"I don't know if that's…" she glanced sheepishly at Dr. Worthy, "I mean, thank you."

"You're welcome, and that is true. If you ever find yourself homesick, I'd love to offer you a position here. As you can see, all of our Egyptologists will be shitting themselves over this for months," she said quietly. "Wherever did you find this anyway? Atef was not forthcoming with too many details. He just mentioned you found it in London."

"In Charles' study, of all places. It belongs to my great aunt now. I…stumbled upon a photo of the tomb when they'd originally discovered it and noted the five jars. He kept journals, but there was no mention of the fifth jar in them anywhere. Strangely enough, I grew up in that study and never even noticed it was there, hidden among the knick-knacks. I happened to be on a Zoom call with my great aunt the other day, and there it was."

"That sneaky bastard," Dr. Worthy chuckled. Stealing an artifact from antiquity doesn't quite fit in with his reputation. Although…"

Elisa's brow rose, "Go on,"

Dr. Worthy hedged a bit. "Well, we have a few of his journals from his later years here in the archives as well. They get a little nutty in some portions. On and on about a ghost in the museum called Neferamun. I guess he got a little senile in his old age."

Elisa tried to cover her shock with a chuckle, but it came out forced. "He was a bit of an eccentric, or so my aunt tells me."

"Would you like to see them? The team has some other work to do, but now that we know what secret Hathor holds, I'd be happy to show you."

Elisa nodded. Charles' journals may not hold the answers she needed, but any opportunity to be closer to Nef, to know him a bit more was one she'd be happy to take.

"And, thank you. For the job offer. I think I'm going to bide my time at the GEM for a while." She shrugged and gave Dr. Worthy a shy smile. "It feels like home."

"Umm, Dr. Kent. I think you might want to see this," Tim called from one of the rooms. His face was pale.

Elisa rushed into a room next to the X-ray machine, where the jar lay on it's back on a soft foam pad for photographing. Underneath it, lay a small, circular piece of the bottom that seemed to have become dislodged.

Elisa looked dismayed. "I don't understand. This looks like a clay coin. Where did it come from?"

She glanced at the disc, which held the inscription of the name of the entombed that had been chiseled away. It looked like it might have fallen out of the bottom of the jar, in which case, there would have been a hole in the jar itself.

"It's a false bottom?" she breathed her stomach in her throat.

When Elisa looked, the jar was still intact. Etched carefully into the original clay were three words.

Tim seemed abashed, "I can't translate it, I'm afraid."

"It says 'Neferamun, the blessed.'"

Sitting in first class was also an opportunity she wasn't going to pass up. Elisa wasn't sure if Atef or New York had provided these particular accommodations, but she was happily sipping champagne and thumbing through Charles's journals while Nef's heart sat in the empty seat next to her.

After the initial shock of seeing Nef's name in writing had passed, Dr. Worthy had allowed Elisa to take the journals with her to read, along with an apology for calling him "nutty." Elisa pretended to be just as struck by the information as she was, unwilling to admit that she had also been communicating with Nef.

Anyone who read these *would* think that Charles had lost all of his marbles. There were detailed notes about conversations with Nef and stories about Nef's Egypt: political affairs, images of certain landscapes, and even a drawing that Charles had done of Nef himself. It was accurate down to the most minute detail. The haughty angle of his jaw, the imposing brows, even the impressive perfection of his toes.

Elisa lingered over that page for far too long. She missed him. Missed having conversations with him in her head. Missed knowing he was always near. She even missed his snarky responses.

Elisa ran her finger along the curve of Nef's drawn lips and her heart stuttered. She missed those, too, if she were perfectly honest with herself. Even if she only felt them for a moment.

Her aunt and Tennyson had been right. It was better to have loved and lost Nef than never to have known him at all.

Now, she would have to steel herself to say goodbye to him once and for all. There was nothing that could convince her to keep him here.

She'd solved the puzzle. Now it was time to ignore her feelings for Nef to do the right thing by him. His name would now go down in the historical record.

She'd called Atef as soon as she could to tell him the news and promised that she'd check the other jars when she got there for other false bottoms.

Elisa had a pretty good idea that the priest who had written the scroll was the same one who took it upon himself to ensure that the right person would find who Neferamun had been, thereby ensuring his entrance into the afterlife.

She glanced to the sky above her and sent up a silent word of thanks to whomever he might have been and hoped that he was enjoying his own version of the afterlife.

The champagne was making her sleepy or the last few days had finally caught up with her. She drifted off to sleep with Nef staring up at her.

"Elisa...Elisa." A voice whispered to her from the wind on the sands.

Elisa found herself standing at the bottom of the giant set of steps again. Her feet were bare, and despite the stars shining above her, the sand was warm between her toes.

The two braziers were lit on either side of her and she could just barely make out the imposing building in front of her. It was most definitely Egyptian; the pillars and lotus murals gave that away, but she'd never seen anything like it herself.

A spotted cat slunk down the stairs toward her, in no seeming hurry.

"Bastet?"

The cat stopped on a wide landing and blinked at her. Elisa would have known those yellow eyes anywhere.

"Elisa..."

The cat's mouth didn't move but she could have sworn there was a distinctive purring sound when her name was called. She looked around for other signs of life but found none.

The cat slowly turned its head to look behind her.

Elisa followed the cat's gaze and saw a woman descending the steps. She had a staff in one hand and was holding a pair of scales in the other. As she got closer, she began to shift. Her feet became paws, while her head began to take on a triangular shape until it became that of a crocodile. Her hindquarters became larger and wider until they resembled a hippo. Elisa wondered briefly how she didn't topple down the stairs, but she was somehow still graceful and steady, though being made of the three most terrifying creatures in all of Egypt made Elisa want to keep her distance.

When the other goddess was in her final form on the landing beside the cat, Elisa could barely breathe.

"Ammit."

The cat was watching her now. Elisa turned back to it and watched as the cat's body transformed into that of a woman but with the cat's head still intact, though larger.

"Bastet...you're actually *Bastet?"*

The cat head nodded and closed her eyes, then her head also transformed into a woman's. She was the most beautiful Elisa had ever seen, with the same yellow eyes and sleek black hair. She wore a circlet around her forehead, and even if Elisa hadn't watched her turn from a cat to a woman, she would have described her movements as feline.

"Have I died?"

Bastet smiled. "No, child, but we must always be prepared."

"I don't understand."

Bastet closed the distance between them, then grabbed Elisa's hands in her own. They were cool against the heat at her feet.

She placed her lips on Elisa's, barely touching them. Her breath smelled like cedar and sandalwood. "When the time comes, you'll know exactly what to do. The words are here." Elisa looked down at the hands that covered her open palms. When Bastet moved her hands from Elisa's, she held one heart in each palm. Bastet brought them to her mouth and whispered something to each of them, in turn. The hearts glowed and then Bastet pressed them both together where they merged into one, pulsating heart.

She placed the heart in Elisa's open palms then gently pressed the heart close to Elisa's chest.

Elisa closed her eyes and felt the warmth of the beating heart against her ribs. Bastet leaned in close to her ear.

"Have faith, my child. Remember...there is always hope."

"Ma'am? Ma'am? We've landed."

The flight attendant leaning over Elisa looked at her expectantly. Elisa turned her head and realized that the rest of the plane was empty.

Chapter Twenty

Elisa tried to gather herself as she hailed a taxi and asked them to take her to the Metropolitan Museum. The driver, not so politely, told her it was closed at this hour, but she insisted.

When they finally got through the chaos of traffic and pulled up, she gaped at the pillars. They resembled the ones of those in her dream with Bastet and Ammit. A chill ran down her spine and she rubbed at the place where Bastet had placed the heart close to her sternum. She'd be happy to never think of the terrifyingly beautiful Ammit again if she didn't have to.

She'd had an email from the curator before her flight left from London that the museum would welcome her, no matter what time she arrived. Still, she'd texted him when she landed to let him know she was on the way. She wasn't about to travel around New York with a priceless and one-of-a-kind artifact in tow.

Elisa walked up the steps and knocked lightly on the glass doors. A banner hung over her head announcing the new Egyptian exhibit, and she smiled when she saw a photograph of Nef's mummy on an advertisement on the door.

An older Asian man with greying hair in a suit approached the doors and smiled at her. He unlocked the one in front of her and she had to step back as he opened it.

"Dr. Kent, I presume?"

"You presume correctly."

He held his hand out to her. "Rick Gionetto. Pleasure to meet you."

"Thank you for having me at such a late hour."

"It's our pleasure. Thank you for sharing this incredible exhibition with us. I was surprised you were willing to head here this evening. Must have been a long flight." He ushered her inside and locked the door behind them.

"I slept most of the way. Besides, I wanted to bring this as soon as I could. Now the collection is complete."

"Atef says it's quite the story."

"It has been."

Mr. Gionetto must have assumed that Elisa wouldn't be terribly forthcoming about it now, so he cleared his throat and gestured to the open doorway on the left.

Egyptian artifacts from Nef's collection and others were encased behind glass, but what struck her most, were the interactive exhibits and the décor. The Metropolitan had taken pains to reimagine Nef's tomb almost exactly as it had been in the photograph. Elisa felt she had stepped through time. It was almost exactly as Nef had shown her in the vision he shared.

"My goodness. This is...incredible."

"We've been working on it for quite some time. This part of the collection from the GEM was the last piece of the puzzle, if you will."

Mr. Gionetto preened a bit as he showed Elisa different aspects of the exhibit.

When they arrived at Nef's sarcophagus, now encased in glass, she stared down at the well-preserved mummy she knew so well. She hadn't though of him as "just a mummy" in so long. This wasn't really the Nef she knew. Her Nef was just as alive as she was.

"It's a shame you could never identify him. The one that got away, hmm?"

Elisa couldn't pull her gaze from Nef's mummified body.

"His name is Neferamun." She said softly. "We made a discovery yesterday at the British Museum. This jar had a false clay bottom. There's a name inscribed on the true base, 'Neferamun the blessed.'"

Elisa? She heard in her head, but it was distant.

Nef, I'm here. Where are you?

Exploring. I'll come down.

Elisa's body warmed at the thought of having Nef near, but her palms grew sweaty knowing what she was ultimately here to do.

She'd tuned out what Mr. Gionetto was saying though she heard something about a press release and updating the signage around the exhibit.

Elisa interrupted him. "Would it be possible to have a minute alone with him? I know that might seem strange…"

"Not at all. Take all the time you need. I'll be in my office, just across the lobby, if you need me. Then we can place the new jar with the others." He nodded at the pedestal across from them where the other four jars sat. The glass had been removed, just waiting for Hathor to join the set.

Mr. Gionetto walked out, his feet tapping across the lobby floors, and Elisa glanced up to see Nef leaning casually against the frame of the doorway.

He looked the same as Elisa remembered, though today, he wore a white polo shirt that pulled around his biceps and khaki slacks that fit too well above his brown penny loafers. Once again, he looked like a millionaire on holiday rather than a ghost.

Nef smiled his half-smile at her as he raked his gaze over her body.

You look good enough to eat. I missed you.

I missed you too.

Did you bring me a present? His eyebrow lifted as he looked at the crate.

In a manner of speaking. Nef walked toward her. *It's your heart.*

He stopped dead in the middle of a pedestal of shabti figures. His chest and arms were visible, but the rest of his body looked encased with everything else. Elisa couldn't help but chuckle at him.

"You found it?" He said aloud. "But how?"

A lot has happened since you've been gone. But this was in Charles' study the whole time.

I don't understand why he would keep it.

Elisa shrugged. *Maybe we aren't meant to, but it's here now. With you.*

Elisa, I don't want to go back. He moved closer to her now, out of the glass case, until her nose was almost at his chest. He tucked her hair behind her ear. Elisa looked up at him and saw the determination in is dark eyes.

Please, Elisa. I've had a lot of time to think. I can stay with you. I can be happy with you like this. I know I said I could let you go, but I don't think I can/

Elisa looked down at the case in her hands. She lowered it to the ground and carefully removed the Hathor jar. She pressed it to her chest, right where Bastet had pressed the joined hearts in her dream. Elisa wondered for a moment if it had been a dream, a vision, or a warning, but it didn't matter. The message to send Nef home had been clear.

You've had a vision with Bastet, he searched her face and her thoughts, *and Ammit?*

I did. And as much as I wish it were true, you don't belong here with me. You deserve peace. Tears threatened on the edge of her lashes, but she willed them away. She knew her path. This puzzle was easy to solve now that she had all of the pieces.

Elisa, I love you.

Elisa stood up on her tip-toes and placed her lips against Nef's. The familiar comfort of the buzz of him seemed to envelop all of her.

She stepped back and pulled the scroll from her pocket. With Nef's heart in one hand and the scroll in the other, she knew she had everything she needed to send him on.

This isn't the reunion I'd hoped for. Elisa, stop, please. Nef reached for her, but while his hands encircled her wrists, she ignored the tingle and opened the papyrus. The tingling intensified and traveled up her arms, through her chest, and into her throat, which tightened a fraction, before her whole body relaxed.

She felt she should have incense or something more sacred than standing in the midst of a museum exhibit, but being in the replica of Nef's tomb somehow felt right.

Elisa glanced at Nef again, her chest constricting. She didn't know if she would get all of the words right, and if she didn't—if she failed—she would hate herself forever for keeping him here.

Bastet, guide me.

Her body stilled and her eyes closed. She felt as though someone was dripping cold water onto her eyes and mouth. She opened her eyes to focus all of her attention on the scroll and began to read.

'I am the benu, the soul of Ra, who guides gods to the Netherworld when they go forth. The souls on earth will do what they desire, and the soul of Neferamun will go forth at his desire.

Elisa's hand began to tremble and if she didn't know better, she'd have thought she was beginning to glow. Her voice rang with power and confidence.

O you gates, you who keep the gates because of Osiris, O you who guard them and who report the affairs of the Two Lands to Osiris every day; I know you and I know your names. My mouth has been given to me that I may speak with it in the presence of the Great God. My mouth is opened, by mouth is split open by Shu with that iron harpoon of his with which he split open the mouths of the gods.'

Nef's hands around her wrists grew tighter and almost painful, but Elisa read on.

O you ba, greatly majestic, behold, I have come that I may see you; I open the Netherworld that Neferamun may see his father Osiris and drive away darkness, for he is beloved of him. I have opened up every path which is in the sky and on earth, for Neferamun is the well-beloved son of his father Osiris. He is noble, he is akh, he is equipped; O all you gods and all you akhu, prepare a path for him.

May he have power in his heart, may he have power in his arms, may he have power in his legs, may he have power in his mouth, may he have power in all his members, may he have power over invocation-offerings, may he have power over water, air, the waters, streams, riparian lands, men who would harm him, women who would harm him in the realm of the dead, those who would give orders to harm him upon earth.

O you gates, prepare a path for Neferamun the Blessed.'

Elisa stared into Nef's eyes. She could feel him as solidly as she could feel the floor under her feet. His fingers were dug so deeply into her skin that she was sure he'd leave bruises.

"It didn't work," she breathed.

"No, but I can feel you, Habiba." He crushed his mouth to hers. Still holding the jar and the scroll, Elisa threw her arms around his neck and pressed her body against his. They were a tangle of tongues and teeth, tasting and savoring one another.

A feminine voice cleared her throat behind them.

Elisa didn't want to pull away, and she wasn't sure how she was going to explain making out with her ghost-boyfriend in the middle of a closed museum to anyone. But when she finally turned her head away from Nef, she realized it wasn't just anyone.

"Bastet," Elisa breathed.

Nef hadn't pulled his gaze away from Elisa, but he said against her cheek, "Hello, little mother."

Bastet laughed. "Did you know it was me all along, Son of Osiris?"

"No, but I knew that cat was something special."

"I'll take that as a compliment," Bastet purred.

She sauntered over to them and rubbed her cheek against Elisa's.

When she was a cat, this seemed normal, but now that Elisa knew she was an actual Goddess, it felt a bit odd.

"What are you doing here, Bastet?" Nef asked as he gently pushed Bastet off of Elisa.

"She asked us to clear a path for you, so I have."

"I don't un—" Nef started.

Elisa interrupted. "She means she's taking you home. To the Afterworld."

"But why am I in this form? With a body, if you're just taking me away?"

Bastet reached up and touched Nef's cheek, searching for something in his eyes.

"You really are Neferamun the blessed. It was a small gift." She shrugged. "Just a moment, but the moment is over and Horus will grow impatient if we linger."

Nef turned to Elisa again and pressed his forehead to hers, tucking her hair behind her ears. "I don't know how many times or how many languages or lifetimes I can tell you I love you, but I hope you know how desperately grateful I am to know you, Elisa Kent."

Elisa couldn't stop the tears from flowing this time. It might have been easier if Nef had just *poofed* after the spell and disappeared, but she would keep the moment she got to hold him in her arms for the rest of this lifetime.

She looked up at him as Bastet moved toward his sarcophagus and smiled. He wiped her tear with his thumb and then kissed her salt-stained cheeks.

"Maybe save a place for me in the afterlife?"

"I hope you aren't there for a long while yet, Habiba, but there will always be a place for you with me."

Nef kissed her forehead one last time, then placed his lips on her eyelids, her nose, her neck, and finally her lips.

"I love you, too," Elisa said through a choked sob.

Nef reluctantly pulled away from her.

Bastet reached out her hand to him. As soon as Nef grasped hers, they were gone.

Chapter Twenty-One

One Month Later

Elisa sat back in her office chair and surveyed the pyramids, glowing in the sunset. The last month had been a blur of interviews, lectures, writing for publications, and who knew what else. She mostly hated it. She'd wanted to make a name for herself, but the exhaustion from dealing with the people was all too real.

Thank goodness for Atef, who had started fielding calls for her. Robert and Tomas had covered a majority of the lab work, which Elisa barely saw these days, and had become interim assistants to her—scheduling meetings, helping with emails, and reporting to her on what they'd accomplished each day.

The first day back at work, she had to stop herself from tearing up every time she entered the lab. She'd cried herself to sleep on more than a few occasions, and tried to remind herself that it was useless to cry over someone who had died long before she'd been born. But it didn't matter. The ache for Nef lingered. Try as she might, she couldn't logic her way out of it.

Being busy helped. She'd known that making a historic find would but her on the map in her own community, but she hadn't realized how fascinated the rest of the world would be as well.

Atef sensed that something was off after her trip to New York. He didn't press, though he'd asked if she was homesick for London a time to two. She assured him she was fine, but he'd caught her drifting out of conversations a few times.

There was a knock on her office door, and she turned around to see Tomas standing there, a stack of papers in hand.

"Come on in, Tomas." She was tired and couldn't muster any enthusiasm for him at the end of another long week.

He entered cautiously. She didn't think she'd been in a mood lately, but she did have much less patience for him these days.

"I just wanted to remind you that you have a meeting with the head of the Egyptian Antiquities council first thing Monday morning."

Elisa glanced down at the notepad she always kept on her. Circled and with stars around it was a note about that.

"I've got it down."

"I also put it on your digital calendar too."

"You know I hate those notifications, Tomas,"

"I know, but I didn't want you to forget."

"I'll head there first and then come into the office. You can hold down the fort in the meantime."

He nodded and looked at the next item on his list.

"Dr. Paoula called. She's going to be in town later this month and wanted to know if you'd like to have lunch."

Elisa didn't have to pretend to smile at that request. "Absolutely. Whenever is convenient for her."

"Got it," he jotted a note on the top piece of paper. "She also wondered if you'd like to come out for the beginning of the next dig season."

"Also, absolutely, yes. If Atef can spare us, let's see if Robert wants to tag along. And you, too, if you'd like."

Tomas raised his eyebrows. Elisa knew she was being uncharacteristically generous with him, but he and Robert had both earned a break from the lab even if it wouldn't be for several months yet.

"Uh, sure. Thank you," he started to make another note.

"I'll talk to Atef about that one."

"Oh, shoot. That reminds me. He wanted to see you in his office. He's interviewing that new assistant director of Egyptology and wanted to introduce you."

"Was he going to talk to me about this?"

"We covered it in the board meeting on Monday," his face paled, "...which you weren't at because you were in a lecture and I forgot to email you the notes."

Elisa had never seen anyone do the facepalm emoji in real life, but Tomas did it now with his free hand and almost stabbed himself in the eye with his pen.

She bit back a laugh. *Would have served him right though,* she thought. She sighed and pushed back from her desk.

"It's okay, but next time you forget, I'm going to make you get me coffee for a month."

"I pretty much do that now, anyway."

"Shall I send you back to Paoula permanently?"

"Nope! Got it."

She moved around her desk and pulled her hair down. She'd been forced out of her usual, comfortable slacks and button-down in favor of a suit and blouse lately because she never knew when Atef might call her into a meeting with someone important. He'd practically made her buy a new wardrobe.

Today's version was a navy pencil skirt with a cream silk blouse. It wasn't uncomfortable, per se, but after a certain time of day, she just couldn't wait to get out of her clothes and be frumpfortable again.

Elisa started walking toward Atef's office, and Tomas stopped her.

"Um, Dr. Kent? Shoes might be helpful."

Elisa looked down at her bare feet. *Isis help me, I'm losing it.*

"Ugh," she said as she passed Tomas to get back into her office. She'd forgotten she even kicked the torture devices that were her heels under her desk.

"If I didn't have you and Robert, I might forget where my own head were if it weren't attached. Thanks, Tomas."

She readjusted her hair over one shoulder and stopped in front of Tomas. "Look okay?"

"Better than okay, Lisa," He grinned.

"Nope! Not today, Tomas, that ship has sailed. But thank you. Go home. Have a nice weekend."

Elisa heard Tomas sigh as she walked down the hall to Nef's office and she rolled her eyes. Maybe he'd meet some girl at a bar and stop trying to ask her out again.

She tapped on Atef's closed door with her knuckles, and when she heard him say, "enter," she peeked her head in. The overwhelming scent of frankincense and sandalwood hit her square in the nostrils. It reminded her so much of Nef, she had a hard time moving forward.

"Ah! Elisa! Just in time."

Elisa entered to find Atef at his desk and a man with his back to her. His hair was dark and long, and even while seated, she could tell he was tall. Something about the breadth of his shoulders in his suit seemed awfully familiar.

"Dr. Elisa Kent, I'd like to introduce you to Dr. Johnathan Watson."

Whatever Atef said after, was lost to the pounding in Elisa's ears, because when the man turned around, she felt like she'd been punched in the stomach.

It was Nef.

His grin was radiant as he met her gaze.

He stood and offered a hand to her, "It's a pleasure to meet you, Dr. Kent. Dr. Tawfik has told me so much about you."

Elisa had no words. Her mouth gaped open and she walked up to him as if in a daze, and reached out for his hand. It was warm and strangely solid. As if he were really alive.

The handshake was awkward, which Atef seemed to notice.

"Everything all right, Dr. Kent?"

Elisa shook her head to clear it and took back her hand, still tingling from Nef/Dr. Watson's touch.

"Yes, it's just…I'm sorry, have we met before?"

Dr.-Nef-Jonathan-Watson glanced at Atef and then at Elisa. "No, I don't believe so. I grew up in London, though, which Dr. Tawfik says you know well, so perhaps we've crossed paths."

He doesn't remember. Or he's not actually Nef.

"Perhaps," Elisa's brain was whirling. Everything in her was telling her this was the love of her life, as a real, alive man, standing in front of her. His voice was the same, his eyes, lips, mouth, nose. But how could any of this be possible?

"I'm sorry, will you just excuse me for one moment?" She backed up and almost collided with the open door. "Back in a jiff."

She practically ran down the hallway to her office. Perched on the arm of the sofa there was Bastet in her cat form.

Elisa about had a heart attack. She hadn't seen her in her cat or goddess form since she'd whisked Nef off to the afterworld.

Her first instinct was to reach out and snuggle her, but she stopped herself. "How did you get in here?"

Elisa realized she would sound like she was talking to herself again, so she closed the door and almost hissed at Bastet.

"Actually, that's beside the point. How did *he*," she said, pointing in the direction of Atef's office, "get here and why in bloody hell doesn't he know who I am?"

Bastet blinked at Elisa, who was almost nose-to-nose with her, and flicked her tail. She shifted for a moment into a tall lioness and then back into a cat before Elisa could blink. Then promptly licked her paw and began cleaning her face.

"Don't go all Sekhmet on me. You're so helpful when I need you to be, and awfully spiteful when I don't."

Bastet cocked her head at Elisa, with her paw still raised, then jumped off the couch and headed for Atef's office.

"No, come back here. You're an awful goddess, but a damned good cat."

Elisa chased her down and tried to stop her before she slank through the door, but Bastet was faster than she was.

"What do we have here?" She heard Atef ask.

Elisa gathered her strength and strode into the office, only to find Bastet rubbing against would-be-Nef's legs like she used to.

"I do apologize," Elisa said.

"Is this a friend of yours," Atef asked.

"In a manner of speaking," Elisa replied, through tight lips. "She disappeared from my home when I was in New York, but it seems she's somehow found me here."

"How wonderful!" Atef rose to greet the cat as pretend-Nef reached down to pet her.

"What's her name?" Elisa was immediately taken back to the first night Nef had joined her at her apartment and asked the very same question. All of the blood drained from her face and she fought against the constriction of her throat.

"B...Bastet," she finally managed to get out.

"Hello, little mother," the amnesiac-Nef said as he scratched her under the chin. "A beautiful name for a beautiful creature."

"Yes, well, I'm thinking about changing it to Apep, in honor of the god of chaos."

Atef chuckled. "Nonsense. She found her way home. Someone must have let her in though. How did she get up here?"

Elisa opened her hands and looked at Atef, "It's a mystery." Elisa walked over to Bastet and bent to pick her up. Her hand grazed Nef's as he continued petting Bastet. "I'd best get her home, though."

Bent at Nef's feet, she looked up to see him looking at her intently. "Maybe we have met somewhere. You suddenly seem very familiar."

There was still no real recognition in his eyes, but Elisa silently willed him to remember her.

Atef cut in, "Well, this is the strangest introduction and interview I think I've ever conducted, but Dr. Watson, with Dr. Kent's consent, the job is yours if you want it."

Elisa stared into Nef's eyes as Bastet purred against her chest. She could so easily get lost in the darkness there. "I consent."

"Excellent!"

Elisa stood up and gathered Bastet more tightly against her. "It was nice to meet you. I'm looking forward to working with you."

"You as well," he said quietly as he returned her stare.

Elisa walked out of the room and back into her own office. She closed the door firmly behind her and dumped Bastet unceremoniously onto the sofa.

"I'll meet you at home. You have some serious explaining to do."

Bastet turned her back on Elisa, then did a quick circle and plopped down with her belly showing.

There was a light knock on her door, and Elisa jumped, then quickly said, "Come in!" more forcefully than she'd intended.

"Dr. Kent? I didn't mean to disturb you." Nef entered cautiously.

Elisa smoothed her blouse and skirt. "It's not a problem. What can I do for you?"

"I just can't shake this strange feeling that I know you. I know this is going to sound strange, but...have I kissed you before?"

Elisa didn't know how to answer. If she admitted to this supposed stranger that they'd done a whole lot more than that, shared more, would he believe her? If she said no, would she ever have a chance to find out if alive-Nef would have feelings for her in a world where they both existed together?

Bastet watched Elisa, caught in the struggle of trying to figure out what to do then looked at Nef. She meowed gently and Elisa felt like the world around her stopped.

Nef moved slowly toward her, but they were no longer in her office. They were in his bedroom. The one he'd shown her in their shared vision. He no longer wore a suit, but the kilt she'd seen him in.

He reached up and ran his knuckles over her cheekbone. Elisa breathed him in and a tear ran down her cheek and landed on his finger.

She bit her bottom lip, unsure of what to say or do.

Nef's lips were inches from hers, but she was immobilized.

He gazed into her eyes again and then gently touched his lips to hers. The tingle that she usually felt when he kissed her was gone, replaced by firm lips that tasted her curiously, cautiously.

He pulled back for a moment and looked at her again, surprised.

"Elisa?"

His eyes now held some sense of recognition in her. "Nef. You remember?"

He closed his eyes and pinched the bridge of his nose. "Sort of. It's all a little foggy...like a dream." He opened his eyes again and traced her lips with his thumb. "But you, I could never forget."

Her lips curved up in a slight smile, "I beg to differ. You did ex—"

Nef stopped her argument with another kiss. "We can talk more about that later. Right now, I only want one thing." His eyes darkened.

Elisa backed up out of his arms a little. "Food?"

"I am hungry," he almost growled, "but not for food."

Elisa felt the moisture pooling already between her legs. She glanced around her office. "Not here. Let's go home."

Chapter Twenty-Two

The taxi ride back to her apartment was almost unbearable. Elisa wasn't about to make out with him in front of their cab driver like a teenager, but Nef couldn't stop touching her, nor she him. It started with small circles of his thumb while they held hands and gazed into each other's eyes, then they'd turned more fully toward each other, their lips only inches apart while he grazed his thumb over her nipple. Elisa tried not to moan in the back seat, but she closed her eyes as his hand slowly traced each rib, then massaged her hip.

He didn't take his gaze from her for a single moment, nor did they say a single word to one another. All Elisa wanted to do was breathe him in and share space with this man who seemed, somehow, to be fully alive and in her arms.

By the time they reached her apartment, she was so wet she was afraid she'd left puddles on her skirt and the car seat. There was a bulge in Nef's pants that he was having a hard time hiding when he closed the car door. He pulled Elisa behind the wall of the stairwell after she'd paid the driver, and immediately buried his head in her neck. He kissed and bit softly while she fisted her hands in his long hair.

His fingers found the hem of her skirt and he slowly pushed it above her thighs.

"I haven't seen anything like this on you before."

"It's a little tight," she said breathlessly.

"But it looks so good on that beautiful backside of yours."

He moved a hand around to her ass and squeezed for emphasis, while his other hand moved higher up her leg. He found the wet spot on her panties and groaned against her collarbone.

"I've already died once, *ma cher*, but you may be the death of me again."

He pushed her legs apart gently, then slid her panties over. Elisa pulled his head to hers to stifle her moans with his mouth while he slowly circled her clit.

She had never done anything like this outside the privacy of a bedroom. She could hear the traffic just on the other side of the stairwell, but her head was so full of Nef, she didn't even care.

"This is how you like it, yes?" The circular movements of his fingers got faster with more pressure. She remembered getting herself off while he'd watched and given her the vision of their bodies entwined.

She moaned against his mouth again and tried to nod, but her orgasm was already coming in fast around her. Her hips and buttocks tensed in anticipation of the relief that was coming. Nef kissed her harder, his tongue echoing the movements of his finger, and Elisa relaxed into him as her lower muscles clenched hard around nothing.

She'd stopped breathing when she came and took in a huge lung of air with Nef's next kiss. "I want..."

"Tell me, Habiba," he kissed her cheeks slowly while his finger still stroked her clit softly. The spasms in her muscles had mostly stopped.

Elisa tried to focus her gaze on Nef. "I want you inside of me."

Nef growled again as he kissed her, then picked her up. Elisa let out a noise of surprise against his lips.

"Let me go!"

"Never." Nef took the stairs two at a time while he carried her up to her door. She was afraid he might break it down while he still held her, but she managed to fish her keys out of her bag. He put her down long enough for her to unlock the door, then pushed her inside and shut and locked it again within a second.

His lips were on hers again as he carried her to the bedroom and set her gently on the bed then straddled her.

"I don't have the words to tell you how much I want you, Elisa, but I intend to take my time with you. I've had centuries of being without a body, but I fully intend to enjoy every moment of this with you."

Nef unbuttoned her blouse at the wrists, then started at her neck and worked her shirt out of her waistband. He sat back on his heels and stared at her in her open shirt and white bra, his finger tracing the skin at the edge of the lace.

"Exquisite," he whispered.

Elisa could see her cleavage bouncing slightly in time with her erratic heartbeat. No one had ever looked at her this way before. She was almost sure he'd devour her if he could have.

Her skirt was still hiked up to her thighs, but he found the zipper at her hip and slid that down then pulled her down further on the bed and wiggled it from her hips until it became a navy pool on the floor.

Nef stood up and removed his suit jacket and tie before unbuttoning his own shirt and discarding it on the floor. Elisa bit her bottom lip and squirmed a little as he undid his belt and pulled it through the loops at his waist.

One eyebrow cocked up. "You like that," he said as more of a statement than a question."

"I didn't know I did until just now. You have such beautiful hands."

He chuckled. "Thank you. I hope there are more things you didn't know you liked that we can discover together." He lifted her leg and bent his head to kiss the instep of her foot and continued up her ankle. "I think I remember that you like this."

Elisa pressed her head down harder into the pillow and moaned. "Mmm. I do."

Nef continued kissing up her leg, to the back of her knee and inner thigh. He nipped at her hip, which made her squirm again, then pressed a kiss to her to her clit, still covered by her panties. He inhaled her scent.

Elisa hadn't felt self-conscious with him until now, but she tried to close her legs against him.

He looked up at her, curious. "You don't like that?"

"It's not that...I just..."

"You smell amazing." He closed his eyes and bent his head to her again, inhaling. "And I bet you taste even better." He sat up and worked her panties down over her hips. "Like fresh cinnamon and spices."

Her panties were discarded with the rest of their clothing and Nef bent his head again to Elisa's inner thigh. He kissed along the tendon there and worked his way slowly, carefully over to her lower lips.

It wasn't that no one had gone down on her before, but it was so far past recent memory that Elisa had almost forgotten how good it felt. All of Nef's attention seemed to be on one thing and one thing only; giving her pleasure. And she was getting it in spades.

She wasn't in a hurry to come again, she simply wanted this feeling of him to last forever. His mouth was warm against her skin and his goatee scratched against the sensitive skin on her thighs, giving her a new sensation to focus on. Her body responded instantly to each new touch of his mouth.

When his tongue finally found her clit, her hips bucked against his mouth, and she clenched the duvet cover underneath her. At first, he was slow and gentle, but the more her cries increased, the more he began to be more demanding. The pressure of his tongue increased until she was on the verge of another orgasm. Elisa was lost to him and to it. Her eyes closed as her hips moved of their own volition against him. She felt the pressure of another orgasm build. Her body stilled as another wave of pleasure moved through her.

Before she could even relax and enjoy the euphoria of the moment, Nef began sucking on her clit while he inserted two fingers into her. Her last orgasm hadn't even subsided yet, but she was already about to lose it again. Her legs shook and she clenched around Nef's fingers while her legs closed in on his head.

She closed her eyes and saw flashes of light as her second orgasm in as many seconds ripped through her, leaving her breathless. She knew she was still on the bed, but it felt like she floated above both of them, completely untethered to anything corporeal.

"I think you just ripped my soul from my body," she panted while he chuckled against her. The vibration from his laugh sent more pleasure skidding down her limbs.

"I could feast on you all day, Habiba. You open so nicely for me, my little lotus."

Elisa's legs still shook, but she crooked a finger at Nef and beckoned him closer. His head rested on her chest as he wrapped his arms around her.

"I can feel your heartbeat," she ran her fingers through his hair.

"I'm surprised," he said, lifting his head and giving her a sly smile, "as most of the blood in my body has traveled lower than my heart."

He kissed her sternum and then inched his way up the rest of her neck until they were face to face. This time, she was the first to lean into him for a kiss and she tasted herself on him. He was right—musky and full of spice and something else more primal.

She reached down between them to get to the button of his pants while he removed her bra and shirt. When he sat up to help her remove his pants, she let out a small gasp. Not only at his size but also that he was circumcised.

"Is something wrong?" He looked down, concerned.

"Not at all. I've seen the historical records of Egyptians practicing circumcision as early as 2300–"

His laugh boomed around the room. "You can make a case study of me later, my love, or ask me the million questions that are constantly on your mind, but right now, *I* have other things in mind."

It wasn't hard to forget everything she thought she knew when Nef kissed her again. She wrapped her hand around him and he moaned then let out a soft curse in his language that she didn't understand as she rubbed the head of his cock against her.

He pushed slowly inside her, his breath already ragged. Elisa wrapped both arms around his shoulders as their bodies adjusted to each other.

"You feel so good, Habiba," Nef bowed his head into her neck as his body began to move in a slow rhythm to their heartbeats. With each thrust, Elisa began to relax a bit more, until she felt so full with him that she thought she might burst. There was a tinge of pain mixed with the absolute joy of feeling him inside of her.

Nef lifted her right leg and bent it at the knee, where he tucked it under his arm and Elisa arched her back off the bed as much as she could with him on top of her. The little bit more depth this gave him was enough to make her feel another orgasm rise. Her moans reverberated around the room, and she drew her nails down his back as the flames inside her built until she was falling off the precipice again. She couldn't breathe and her body stilled as she rode the wave of yet another climax.

Nef slowed his pace, and breathed in her ear, "May I get behind you?"

Elisa nodded, though she wasn't fully aware of what was happening. She let Nef turn her over. She felt a little too exposed with her ass up in the air in front of him, but he caressed her cheeks gently and then squeezed.

"Put your arms underneath you, Habiba," he leaned down and guided her arms where he wanted them. On hands and knees, Elisa felt a little less vulnerable.

"Your whole body is a wonder, but there's something about this back side of yours that I just can't get enough of," he said as he pressed against her. "This curve of your hips," he said as he traced his fingers over each side, "to this delicate dip at your waist."

Elisa practically purred under his touch and at his words. It was a revelation to be seen this way. As beautiful, as desirable.

Nef pulled her hips back toward him and entered her again. If she'd felt full before, now she was overflowing.

"That's my girl. Arch your back for me."

She pushed up more on her hands, and Nef pulled her head back gently by her hair to get her in the position he wanted.

"There," he growled as he thrust inside her.

Her body didn't feel like her own. She was floating again on a high of ecstasy and never wanted to come down. After only a few minutes she was beginning to shatter again. Her muscles clenched hard around him and Nef pulled her toward him, harder, by the hips, and with her name on his lips, Elisa felt him empty himself inside of her.

Hours and many orgasms later, Elisa lay wrapped in Nef's arms. He was dozing, and she rubbed his back and counted his heartbeats every now and then to reassure herself that this wasn't a dream. How did this happen, though? Why was he back? Why hadn't he remembered her? If he had, surely he would have come straight back here and not left her to pine for him for the rest of her life.

"I can hear you thinking, Elisa," he whispered, and his lips cocked in a smile.

Her eyes went wide. "You can still hear my thoughts?"

He shook his head, "No, unfortunately, but I can still hear your brain turning."

"I'm just curious…as to how you got here."

"We took a taxi."

Elisa rolled her eyes at him. "You know what I mean."

"Well, before that, I took a plane from London to Egypt."

"Neferamun, be serious."

He looked a little stunned. "I've never heard you use my whole name before. I like it." He snuggled her closer and kissed her forehead. "I also like to get you riled up."

"I've noticed."

"Shall I rile you in a different way already? Are you not yet satisfied?" He wiggled his hips at her.

Elisa laughed. "Please, no. I'm not going to be able to walk tomorrow." She looked up at him and gave him her best impression of a puppy with big eyes. "Please just tell me."

"It's still a little fuzzy, to be honest. Like a dream I'm trying to remember, but only getting fragments of."

"A puzzle then. Let's sort it together. I've got nowhere to be today."

"Fine. After Bastet took me away, I remember seeing Osiris, he sent me to The Hall of Judgment. I remember being terrified of the forty-two sets of eyes glaring at me from around the room. I had to confess to anything I'd done or not done in life.

"'I did not lie,' 'I did not steal,' 'I did not kill,'" He interrupted himself, "I had to work around that one a bit as I did kill people in the name of my kingdom in life, but it was an acceptable amount to the Judges, it seems."

"Then Osiris weighed your heart against Maat, the feather of truth on the scales."

"Do you want to tell this story, or shall I?"

She chuckled. "Sorry. Do go on."

"Well…you're right. And he did. Ammit was bloody terrifying, by the way."

"I remember. I met her."

"I forgot. In a vision, yes?"

"Something like that." Elisa remembered the vision of Bastet joining two hearts together and shivered. "Get back to your story."

Nef settled in again. "You seem to know most of it. But when Osiris declared my heart 'true of voice,' a door opened to the Field of Reeds. I saw my family there, my friends. I knew I'd found everything I'd wanted. But Bastet strode through with Neferaue. This is where it gets a little more fuzzy. I remember my anger. Bastet asking her if she'd been the one to poison me. Neferaue dropped to her knees and confessed, I think. Then Ammit ate her heart and she disappeared.

"This part, though, is very clear: Bastet and Osiris gave me a choice. They said since I had been wronged in my first life, I could have a chance at a second one or take my place in the Field of Reeds forever." He looked at Elisa and rubbed her shoulder, "The choice was an easy one. I knew, somehow, that I could find you again."

"Good thing you didn't get sent back as a baby. I would have had to wait twenty years for you to find me."

"I would have loved you even if I was a strapping young man and you an old woman."

"Oh, hush," she said and almost pushed him off the bed as he grinned.

"Fortunately, I woke up, in this time, in my body, in London, but I had no memory of who I'd been. I had the memories of the life of Dr. Johnathan Watson, pictures on the wall, degrees in frames, a life as if I'd always lived it."

"How strange."

"Indeed. Then one day, I got an email inviting me to apply for a job as the associate director of the GEM. I thought it was a hoax at first, but Dr. Watson seemed to have always wanted to go to

Egypt, so I applied, then got the call to come visit for an interview. I didn't remember anything about being...me..until you kissed me."

"I think you kissed me, sir."

He grinned again, "Either way, it was like being slapped in the face with cold water."

"I think you mean 'splashed'," she corrected gently.

"I meant what I said. When will you stop questioning me, woman?"

"Never." Elisa suddenly frowned. "This...life you somehow stepped into...You didn't have a wife or children or...anything did you?"

"No, not that I recall. I mostly just went to work, ate, and came home, like a normal, boring bachelor would these days."

"Mostly?"

He shrugged a shoulder, "I went to a bar or two...but I didn't take anyone home if that's what you're thinking."

"I wasn't," she said quietly.

"Now who is lying? Besides, that would be disloyal, and we're married. I never liked the idea of multiple wives."

"What do you mean, we're married?"

"In my culture, we didn't have marriage as a ceremony with all of the money you people spend on it, in a temple with guests. A couple decided they wanted to be together and started living together...and sleeping together," he waggled his eyebrows at her.

"But we don't live together."

"You snuck me home, where we resided in the same space—here and in the dig house—and we saw each other naked *and* I pleasured you. What would you call that?"

"Dating."

He deflated a bit. "You said you would keep me."

"In my culture, you ask someone if they want to be married."

"Does that mean we have to do the whole ceremony in a church with guests and gifts and such?"

"Does that mean you're going to ask me to marry you?"

"Why should I, when as I said, we're already married?"

"You're insufferable." She pushed away from him and tried to get out of bed.

Nef pulled her back in and tucked her into his side. "But you love me anyway, as I do you." Nef snuggled her even closer and kissed her on the nose.

"You know," she started, hesitantly. "In my vision with Bastet, she showed me two hearts, then joined them and placed them both in my hands. She whispered something to them. What do you think that means?"

Nef's eyebrows rose and then his brow furrowed again. "I don't know. But I think it means that our hearts are now entwined. Maybe I was pulled to you because of her. Either way, you saved me." He rubbed his finger down the tip of his nose as she stared up at him. "Will you be the keeper of my heart, Elisa Kent?"

Elisa sighed happily and snuggled back into him, "Until the serpent eats the sun."

Epilogue

Seven Months Later

It took Elisa less than fifteen minutes to pack. Nef had been packing for a week and was still running around the apartment looking for things to take in his already overstuffed backpack.

"You used to live in practically one outfit thirty-five hundred years ago. How many shirts can you possibly need? We're only going to be gone for four days."

He popped his head out of the doorframe to their bedroom. "Have you seen my blue shirt with the white buttons?"

"Yes, you washed it and packed it four days ago. Come on, the car is going to be here any minute."

Elisa rubbed her hand down the back of their sleeping kitten, Zahi, and he purred and stretched his toes out without waking.

"Does Ashraf know what time to come and feed Zahi?"

Elisa rolled her eyes as her phone dinged to alert her that their car was there.

"You told him four times yesterday, and he messaged both of us this morning to confirm. The car is here."

Elisa heard cursing and something large fell to the floor.

Nef came out, hair pulled back but falling out of his hair tie, backpack falling from his shoulder. She'd never seen him this frazzled.

"Are you okay?"

His face lit up. "Yes, Habiba, just excited."

The dig season had finally started again and Paoula had asked both of them to join her. Robert and Tomas would also be joining them. Asraf, their newest assistant at the lab, would be taking care of their cat and the lab while they were all away.

"Come on, we don't want to miss our flight."

Nef walked over to the couch and kissed Zahi on the forehead. The kitten placed his paw on Nef's face and then licked his nose.

"We're sure this one isn't also a god in cat's clothing, yes?" Nef asked Elisa.

"No. He's not." She glanced at the kitten again, "Pretty sure anyway."

Elisa pulled Nef to the car downstairs. She was thankful he had some time to decompress on the flight south. She was determined not to let him have any more coffee today, though.

She glanced at him as they finally got settled on the plane. It had taken some getting used to to refer to him as "Dr. Watson" at work. She'd chuckled the first few times she'd said it, but it was finally becoming easier.

They'd managed to keep their relationship at the lab a secret for the first few months until Atef had found them making out in her office. He'd been thrilled that Elisa was "getting a life" and chalked it up to love at first sight or destiny, depending on the day.

Not long after, Elisa had finally consented to joining Atef and his family for dinner—at Nef's prodding. Relaxing into Cairo had been a challenge but having Nef by her side made everything easier. He'd almost had a few slip-ups about his past, but he deftly avoided talking about his life as Dr. Watson as much as possible in mixed company and stayed as close to the truth as he could.

His "degrees" in linguistics had been invaluable to their team so far and he'd managed to translate several inscriptions with ease into multiple languages for the GEM. Atef was very pleased with his work.

Nef and Elisa didn't often see each other during the day, but back at home, she'd come to him with a puzzle to solve and he was always ready to give an anecdote or story from his own time to help her. He wasn't much help with anything that came after the time of his death—he'd never seen many of the later temples of the New Kingdom finished—and he couldn't solve the mystery of the Sphinx since it had been built well before his time, but on most things related to his past way of life, he was forthcoming and happy to share.

There were many things he'd been unhappy about: the way a scroll had been translated, how the afterworld was depicted, the way modern society interpreted and interacted with the pyramids, but Elisa reminded him on many occasions that they couldn't just revolutionize Egyptian archeological facts overnight.

She smiled at him as he caught up on his newest obsession on his own phone: regency romances on streaming services.

There were many things she'd regretted in her life, but she didn't regret sending him to the afterlife. There wasn't a day that passed that she didn't send a silent prayer of thanks to Osiris and Bastet for sending him home to her.

The sun was just beginning to set over the horizon when they landed. Paoula had volunteered to come pick them up and take them to the dig house since she'd be taking someone else to the airport as well. She leaned against her old truck and waved at them as she saw them approaching.

Elisa jogged the distance between them, hugged her, and kissed her on both cheeks.

"Paoula, may I introduce Dr. Johnathan Watson to you?"

Nef kissed Paoula's cheeks and clasped her hands, "Buenas noches, Dr. Paoula. ¿Cómo estás?."

"Hola," she said, surprised.

Elisa pointed her thumb at him, "Linguist. He's learning Spanish now."

"Impressive," Paoula smiled. "Bien, gracias. It's nice to finally meet you, Dr. Watson."

Nef was full of questions when they got in the car about what to expect, what they were looking for, what she needed help with.

Elisa tuned them out. Nef loved to talk and that served her well, so she could just fade into the background. He was charismatic and sociable. Happier and more relaxed in life than he had been in death, which, Elisa supposed, was to be expected.

She leaned her head against the cool glass of the door. Temples and pyramids rose out of the sands around her.

"This isn't the way to the Valley," she realized aloud.

Nef and Paoula exchanged a glance.

"No," Paoula said looking ahead. "We're making a detour. Dr. Watson mentioned he hadn't seen Luxor, so I thought we could show him before we get to work."

Elisa scoffed in her head. Of course Nef had *seen* it, it just hadn't been finished in his lifetime. No one could have missed it traveling up or down the Nile. It was twenty-five minutes in the wrong direction, but Elisa didn't mind. Luxor never ceased to fascinate her. She closed her eyes and napped the rest of the way.

She felt the car stop and opened her eyes to see a few stars glimmering and a full moon overhead. Luxor was even more beautiful in the moonlight.

Nef got out of the passenger seat and opened Elisa's back door. He stood with a bag in his hand that she hadn't noticed before. He reached his hand out to her to help her climb out. Paoula remained in the driver's seat.

"Aren't you coming?" Elisa asked.

"No, I thought you could show him around." She smiled.

"There's not much to see at night, but okay."

Elisa hopped down, her hand in Nef's and he closed the doors behind him. They walked a little way, and when she was sure they were out of earshot, she said, "You are such a liar. I know you've been to Luxor."

Nef grinned, sheepishly. "I have. But not all of it. Isn't it beautiful?"

Elisa stared at the massive temple in front of them. "It's what made me want to be an Egyptologist."

Nef raised his eyebrows in surprise. "You never told me that. I thought it was because of your parents."

"Partly. Luxor was my playground when I was four. My parents were here a lot, studying all of the inscriptions," she gestured to the chiseled walls and columns that were covered in hieroglyphs. "This place holds all of my first memories."

"It was only a temple when I was young," Nef said as the continued to walk. "I wish I could still show you, but none of the hieroglyphs were finished the last time I saw it."

Nef had pulled her along to the riverbank of the Nile. He set down the bag he was holding and then pulled out two clay lotus blossoms, each with a candle inside. Then he retrieved a lighter from his pocket.

"I know this is an old custom, but the moon is full, and I thought you'd like to join me."

Elisa was more moved than she could say. Her heart beat only for this man and she would wish for him in this lifetime and every one thereafter.

"It would be my honor."

He lit her candle first, then his. It illuminated his face in a way that made her soul feel whole. They walked to the very edge of the riverbank. He said a prayer in Egyptian, then motioned Elisa to bend down to the water with him. He stood in front of her, placed his clay lotus in first, closed his eyes, and then sang a song she didn't recognize. She'd have to get him to translate it for her.

His voice echoed on the water after the ripples and it seemed the sounds of the animals and insects along the bank stilled. His candle flame flickered a bit as the current carried the lotus down the river, but it stayed lit. He stepped back while he continued his song and motioned for Elisa to release her lotus, too.

She closed her eyes. The September air was almost chilly, but the candle's flame had warmed the clay around it. She placed it in the water, willing it to float, then made a new wish: *I wish for him. Always for him.*

Elisa watched the current carry her lotus away, still floating on the surface, stalwart and steady. Nef had truly been her gift from the gods and she hoped they'd keep it that way.

When she turned around, Nef was on one knee with a box opened in each of his hands.

The ring in the right box was a brilliant carnelian with lapis and amethyst overlapping in the center. It resembled the neckpiece she'd first seen him in. He was grinning from ear to ear. The box in his left hand held the heart scarab.

"Dr. Elisa Kent, I come to you on the banks of the Nile, and ask that you be my *official* wife. You have held my heart since the moment I met you. Will you continue to do so now and even into the afterworld?"

Elisa thought about arguing with him, the way he always did with her when this topic came up, but she was too happy to do anything but say yes.

She must have thought a little too long because Nef's face fell. "Dammit, woman, I can't read your mind any–"

She stopped him with a kiss. She pulled away from him and looked at his moonlit face. He'd walked away from the peace of the afterlife to come home to her.

"I would be honored to be your wife in body, mind, and spirit. You'll have me for as long as you want me."

"In this life and the next, Elisa."

"Until the serpent eats the sun," they said in unison.

The End

Thank you so much for reading, *The Feast of the Lotus!* If you enjoyed the book, please consider leaving a review and please follow me on Instagram or subscribe to my newsletter if you want to see more of what I'm working on.

If you loved Elisa's bestie, Miriam, there's a spinoff book coming about her adventures with an Irish ghost in Louisiana, called *The Oracle of Magnolia Place.* You can read a sample on the next few pages.

The Oracle of Magnolia Place

Chapter One

What the actual fuck am I supposed to do with this? Miriam dropped her bags at the end of the cracked sidewalk that led up to the once beautiful sleeping porches. Benedic, her larger-than-life mutt loped up to the steps, sniffing everything with his tail wagging and his tongue lolling out of the side of his mouth.

At least someone is happy. While it would have been the right thing to do to collapse in a heap in her luggage and cry, it wasn't the Limehouse thing to do. But she did pout a little while she gathered herself and her bags and wandered up the catawampus steps. The top one groaned, wanting to buckle under her, so she hopped off of it and to the door as quickly as she could.

She looked up at the years of mildew on the haint blue porch roof. That column was falling off and the gutters were hanging menacingly over the overgrowth on the left side of the house. Some kind of vine was trying to infiltrate the window on the opposite end of the porch. She'd seen worse, but not much.

The screen door creaked just like they do in scary movies when she flung it open and set her duffle down to dig her keys out of her pocket. *It had to be a friggin' skeleton key.* She had laughed that omen off when the package had arrived two weeks ago, but now, standing here, the cold metal carried a foreboding with it that she couldn't seem to shake.

She let out a breath with the *click* of the latch and turned the iron knob. Nothing. *Couldn't be that easy.* Miriam took a deep breath in and shoved her shoulder into the big wood door. It whooshed inward almost as if it had been pulled when she pushed. As a result, she had to catch herself before she landed face-first on the dusty wooden floors. Benedic clambered in behind her, chasing reflections and dust motes. Thankfully here, there was nothing for him to run into. His paw prints were left in the thick dust of the entryway, and she smirked to herself as she was suddenly reminded of the magical footprints left behind on a magical map in one of her favorite YA books.

At least there would be room for her books here. She scanned the room and noted the fireplace. It was a pretty enough little house, right off the bayou in Terrebonne Parish, Louisiana. Which she had absolutely no interest in. She missed her condo in Charleston already. But, a promise was a promise and she had promised her father she'd come down, flip the house, and go home; hopefully a whole lot richer.

She wandered into the old kitchen while she thought about the life she'd make with the money from this place. Anything would be better than the last six years, and better still, the last six months. It seemed like everything she touched turned to ash. In such a short time she'd lost clients, her marriage, and, worst of all, her mom and best friend. Her father had given her grace and forgiveness through all of her turbulence and personal drama, but he seemed almost too fond of the chance for his only daughter to be knocked off her high horse and galivanting around the world to go to the middle of nowhere and fix up the house that had been left to her through her estranged grandmother.

Miriam had flickering images of the woman she'd been named after, but nothing that stuck. A smile here, a song there, and somewhere in the back of her mind candlelight and wailing. She hadn't been in this house in thirty years, at least, but it still felt just as old and mysterious as it had back then. Here in the kitchen, herbs and warm candle wax seemed to waft from nowhere and everywhere. Miriam imagined the hundreds, maybe thousands of meals her grandmother had made on this butcherblock countertop. She skimmed her hand over a few of the old knife wounds and chucked to herself at the secrets she knew this house must have.

A knock at the door made her jump. Benedic happily bark-howled in greeting to whomever he had encountered. She rolled her eyes heavenward. *Worst guard dog ever.*

Miriam peeked around the door to see a very handsome man in sunglasses and what looked like an expensive suit standing on the porch. He had an ostentatious bouquet in his hands and he looked completely out of place on the worn planks and overgrown flora.

"Hello? Can I help you?"

He turned and his smile almost knocked her over. He virtually threw the flowers out to her in his exuberance.

"Yes, ma'am. I'm Todd Broussard. Everyone calls me T-Todd since my daddy is also Todd."

She guessed he was in his forties, and as he took off his sunglasses, she noticed lines on his eyes that she felt sure were there from years of practicing that deadly smile. She realized he was looking at her, probably waiting for her to offer up her own name, but she had suddenly forgotten it.

Benedic sniffed her flowers and she came back to herself. "I'm Miriam Limehouse. Nice to meet you."

She rested the flowers in the crook of her arm and awkwardly stuck out her hand from under the bundle for him to shake. He took it and bent over her hand. He brushed warm and soft lips over her knuckles. In her three decades, plus, she had never had someone kiss her hand. All of the hairs on her arm and the back of her neck stood up. A piece of wood fell off the shingling of the house and T-Todd stiffened, chuckled lightly, and stood up, releasing her hand.

"I just wanted to welcome you to the parish. I live a few miles down the road past all the sugar cane. Do you need any help settling in?"

Miriam wondered casually if all the men in this parish were this tall, handsome, and helpful. Then realized she'd said just that out loud.

T-Todd laughed. "Helpful, yes. But not quite as tall or handsome, no." The smile was back.

Embarrassment lodged itself like a stone in her throat and she had to clear it a few times before she could speak. "Ah. Well. Thank you, but no. The house is still mostly furnished and I've got a truck full of supplies coming tomorrow, and a whole crew next week.

"Sounds like you won't be alone out here for long. Still. If you need anything, why don't you give me a call? If you have your phone, I can just put my number in for you."

Maybe she would like it here after all. All of the plans she had been thinking about earlier in the kitchen now suddenly included this smile and this man. She handed him her phone and chuckled when he put his last name in as *tall, handsome, helpful.* As if she'd forget.

"Thank you for stopping by. I hadn't even been in here five minutes when you knocked. Excellent timing."

"You're the talk of the parish. It's not often we get an outsider in this part of the world. Everyone sure did love your Grandmama though."

Miriam had the feeling she was being watched, and not by the handsome man in front of her. She glanced at the shingle that had fallen off the side of the house a moment ago. It seemed to be vibrating ever so slightly. *Shit.* Not the first impression she wanted to make. She forced her attention back to T-Todd.

"If you'll excuse me. I need to try to get unpacked. It's been a long day. And I need to get these in water."

"Of course. I'm sure you want to get settled in. Just holler if you need anything, hear?"

She smiled at him, knowing her smile wasn't nearly as radiant as his. "I will do that. Thank you again."

Miriam watched him get into his very large BMW and drive away before she turned to the kitchen to try to find a vase big enough for the bouquet. As the water filled the pretty stoneware pitcher, she realized that there were some things she hadn't been able to leave behind in Charleston.

Acknowledgments

When working on historical fiction, it's easy to get caught up in the research, but my sweetheart kept me going. Thank you, WHS, for your unwavering belief in me, accountability, and support. Many, many thanks to my beta readers, Alicia Ellis and Joy Eckert, for their invaluable feedback while working on this book.

And to you, dear reader. We writers wouldn't exist without you. Thank you, always, for your support and encouragement. It means the world to us while writing in our hobbit holes.

About the Author

Caroline Smith graduated from Queens University of Charlotte with an MFA in Creative Writing and got her BA from Pacific Lutheran University in English Literature and a minor in Publishing and Printing Arts. While there she fell in love with editing manuscripts and storytelling. She has edited over 500 manuscripts and, in collaboration with one of her authors, won an IBPA Gold Ben Franklin Award for excellence in editorial and design.

When she's not writing or editing, she enjoys reading romance novels and dark fantasy and creating workshops on meditation and natural wellness. She splits time between a small farm in North Georgia and a home in North Carolina, always with her sweetheart, three wild and wonderful children, and a menagerie of animals.

Find out more at www.editorcaroline.com